Alien Night

ON

Union Station

EarthCent Ambassador Series:

Date Night on Union Station

Alien Night on Union Station

High Priest on Union Station

Spy Night on Union Station

Carnival on Union Station

Wanderers on Union Station

Vacation on Union Station

Guest Night on Union Station

Word Night on Union Station

Party Night on Union Station

Review Night on Union Station

Family Night on Union Station

Book Night on Union Station

LARP Night on Union Station

Book Two of EarthCent Ambassador

Alien Night on Union Station

Foner Books

ISBN 978-1-948691-04-8

Copyright 2014 by E. M. Foner

Northampton, Massachusetts

One

"In conclusion, it is the view of Union Station Embassy that the rapid expansion of coeducational classes for human and Stryx children has not gone unnoticed by potentially aggressive species who oppose the galactic status quo, and that the suspected kinetic impact asteroid attack on Earth was—oh, Dorothy!" Kelly interrupted her weekly report for EarthCent to stare horrorstruck at the dripping white mess with a shock of red hair that teetered into her office.

"I'm a mummy too!" Dorothy proclaimed gleefully. "Now I say when to eat ice cream."

"No, Dorothy Anne McAllister. It doesn't work that way," Kelly told her four-year-old daughter while struggling to maintain a look of stern parental disapproval. "Where's Chastity? I'm never letting her babysit again!"

"Blythe said!" Dorothy objected fiercely, a magic formulation that carried the weight of law in her universe.

"Blythe said what?" Kelly asked with a sigh, knowing that Dorothy viewed Chastity's older sister as more of an authority figure than a mere EarthCent ambassador, who just happened to be Dorothy's mother.

"Blythe said she can make me a mummy! Chassy said is not the same thing, but I wanted." The little girl looked pleadingly at her mother as the runny paste pooled at her feet and the long, white strips of paper began to peel and droop with her movements.

Kelly knelt in front of Dorothy and began removing the rest of the sodden strips of paper-maché from her little body. Where did Donna's girls ever find so much paper? Dorothy stood perfectly still once Kelly began the clean-up operation, but it took more than some wet bits of cellulose to dampen her inquisitive spirit.

"Why can't I be a mummy? Metoo is four and nobody tells him nothing."

"Nobody tells him anything," Kelly corrected her. Then she tried again to explain the difference between human children and the little robots to her daughter, who related to the Stryx children as if they were just clever kids made of metal. "Metoo is the same age as you, but he remembers things from long before your Mummy was born. I meant, Mommy. And mummies and mommies are not the same thing. Blythe was making a joke about the way I speak."

"Bad Blythe!" Dorothy said with a pout, but Kelly knew that her daughter would soon forgive Blythe for misleading her, just as she had a dozen times before. Part of Dorothy's admiration for Blythe came from the fact that Donna's seventeen-year-old daughter was dating Paul, and Dorothy positively idolized her older stepbrother.

"Where is Chastity?" Kelly tried asking again. "You didn't come all the way here by yourself."

Dorothy pointed her newly freed arm at the doorway, indicating that the girls were outside. Kelly sprang for the door, which slid open to reveal an empty office. The part-time staff had already cleared out for the weekend, and the only sign of the girls was a bit of a mess on the floor near the kitchenette sink that the maintenance bot would take care of eventually.

"I'll never understand how those girls ended up in the babysitting business," Kelly exclaimed to herself, as Dorothy scampered happily around the office, leaving a trail of dried flecks of flour paste.

"Are you talking to yourself again or were you expecting an answer?" Libby inquired unannounced through Kelly's implant. The Stryx were normally fastidious about respecting the protocols of communications, even though they had a complete disregard for the privacy of EarthCent employees and eavesdropped freely on their human friends. But when Kelly was out on maternity leave four years earlier, she had given the station librarian permission to speak to her without chiming first. The agreement for the diplomatic grade implants that came with Kelly's ambassadorial position allowed the Stryx to monitor her closely in any case, so Libby wouldn't interrupt if she was doing anything important.

"I meant it rhetorically, but I wouldn't mind an answer," Kelly replied out loud. She had cut way back on subvocing since becoming a wife and mother, and she figured it could only help Dorothy to hear English spoken, even when it was only one half of the conversation. "Did you see what those girls did to my little angel?"

"Of course," Libby replied, shifting her voice to the room speakers. "I'm always monitoring what goes on in the embassy office. They originally planned to make her into an angel, but the wire they brought to form the wings wasn't stiff enough, so they gave up and made her a mummy instead. I'm afraid Blythe took advantage of your daughter's limited vocabulary, but it was all in good fun."

"All in good fun? Babysitting isn't supposed to be about fun. It's supposed to be about safety!"

"Really? Then it is surprising that their InstaSitter business is doing so well," Libby replied dryly. "Did you know that they pay me a percentage to let them use the Eemas system for bookings? Operating a babysitting service is practically the same as running a dating service, except the babysitter gets paid, of course."

"If that's all there is to it, I suppose you'll be running an escort service next," Kelly retorted. "That would really be popular, but you might get in trouble with some of the more established guilds."

"InstaSitter is proving to be a fine idea for a business," Libby continued, ignoring the sarcastic comment from the EarthCent ambassador. "It's tremendously popular with many of the station species whose young require supervision. There's already been a noticeable uptick in the restaurant and entertainment business in those sections, and Gryph predicts the knock-on benefits could eventually add several points to the station's economic output. In fact, I'm betting it will lead to a baby boom among the cultures that had no tradition of hired babysitting."

"But they're such horrible babysitters," Kelly protested. "When Dorothy was still in diapers, they used to take her out at night as a prop to increase their flower sales in front of the cafes!"

"And didn't it help their profits?" Libby asked, apparently puzzled by Kelly's complaint. "In any case, they're too busy managing InstaSitter to take any of the babysitting assignments themselves, and most of the clients require non-human sitters."

"Wait. Are you telling me that they only babysit for me as a favor? I thought at two creds an hour, I was giving them a chance to earn real money," Kelly grumbled, as she pulled Dorothy onto her lap. The girl had completed her exploration of the office and the paste had all flecked off of her stain-resistant jumper by this point. Kelly acknowledged to herself grudgingly that no harm had been done and that Dorothy had probably learned a new vocabulary word that she wouldn't forget.

"The minimum rate charged by InstaSitter is four creds an hour, but of course, eighty percent of that goes to paying the sitters, and most of the rest goes to overhead. The girls are very focused on growing their brand rapidly, so they aren't paying themselves salaries yet, but they've already turned down buyout offers that would make them…"

"I don't want to know," Kelly interrupted, putting her hands over her ears like a child. "Can we talk about my weekly report? I'm worried about a connection between Union Station and that suspected asteroid attack on Earth. Is there any data that wasn't shared with the public?"

"Of course," Libby replied. "As reported, it appears that an unknown party was able to redirect a city-sized rock from the asteroid belt between Mars and Jupiter to a course that would have intercepted Earth's orbit in a little over a year. The asteroid contained enough iron content to be manipulated with magnetic projectors, and the residual magnetic polarization demonstrates beyond a doubt that this was an intentional act."

"Right. All of that was reported. So what's been held back?"

"EarthCent alerted the Stryx when the asteroid first appeared on the NEOD, or Near Earth Objects Detection system that we provided to Earth after budgetary constraints had led your governments to abandon their own project. A Stryx science vessel that was sent to tow the asteroid back to its original position was tasked to first ascertain the asteroid's mass and trajectory to a high degree of accuracy. Then it time-synced with the NEOD equipment in Earth orbit and projected the exact location that the asteroid would have entered Earth's atmosphere."

"And?" Kelly prompted impatiently, as Dorothy showed signs of becoming fidgety about something.

"It's impossible to project the precise impact point on Earth's surface, of course, since the atmospheric density is dependent on the local weather, which we can't predict that far out in the future," Libby continued apologetically. "Atmospheric conditions will also have a small affect on how much of the asteroid's crust would burn up on entry, though the analysis showed that the core would have survived without breaking up in any scenario."

"It sounds to me like you're talking about something on the same order as what finished off the dinosaurs," Kelly speculated nervously.

"The kinetic energy released would have been suspiciously similar to that of what your scientists call the K-Pg extinction event," Libby confirmed.

"Suspiciously? You mean somebody has done this before?" Kelly asked incredulously.

"It's hard for us to attribute motivations to unknown actors, especially when they are likely to be biological agents. But due to the obvious nature of the attack and the unlikely choice of weapon, we believe somebody was trying to convey a message."

"You mean a warning," Kelly translated.

"Yes. And that brings us back to the impact location, since anybody going to such elaborate pains to send a warning would probably intend it for a specific audience."

"But I thought you just said that you couldn't accurately determine where it would have hit," Kelly objected.

"I said we couldn't project the precise impact location," Libby countered. "With an asteroid this size it hardly makes a difference in terms of the damage it would have done, and if it wasn't so suspicious, we wouldn't have bothered with all of the math."

"I'm beginning to think you've been taking drama lessons from Jeeves," Kelly interjected impatiently. "What country was it aimed at?"

"Oh, we can do a little better than that. While it's always possible that whoever redirected the asteroid was just settling for hitting Earth, we're working on the assumption that it was carefully aimed. And the target was..." Libby paused dramatically.

"Bubbalo," Dorothy shouted proudly.

"Bubbalo?" Kelly asked, looking from her daughter to the ceiling, where her eyes always tended to drift when talking with Libby.

"Bubbalo," Dorothy repeated, emphatically. "Libby teach'ed me."

"Buffalo," Libby corrected her gently.

"As in Buffalo, New York?" Kelly began to rise, before thinking better of it and depositing Dorothy on the floor. "You're getting too big for me to carry, Sweetie."

"Yes. We haven't come up with any high probability matches for targets in Buffalo, although if our theory is correct, the targeted entity might be able to identify the threat if we publicly announced everything I just told you."

"I'm not sure how wise that would be," Kelly speculated, taking Dorothy's little hand and leading her towards the corridor. "There's not much point to panicking people into abandoning a city when the asteroid would have wiped out everybody on the planet, whoever it was aimed at. And you've already admitted that they might have just pointed it at Earth without doing all of the extra math."

"That's the consensus of EarthCent staff, which is why we limited the details in the public release. We've stepped up the monitoring of Earth space for potential threats, and EarthCent has been funded to install the latest biological threat sensors."

"Well, I have to get this munchkin home for our family-night meal. It took me forever to talk everybody into the idea, so it wouldn't look good if I missed it. I'd like to discuss this more later, but please let me know immediately if you see any evidence to tie the asteroid attack to the Stryx school on Union Station."

"Enjoy your family night," Libby said. "Bye bye, Dorothy."

"Bye, Aunty Libby," Dorothy replied, adding a vague wave at the space behind her. The girl still had trouble grasping that Libby didn't have to be in the same room to speak to her, and she assumed that Libby was a big version of Metoo who was always hiding behind the furniture.

Walking slowly to match her pace to Dorothy's little steps, Kelly headed for the lift tube closest to the embassy offices. The reduced rate of progress gave her time to pay attention to the ceiling-high corridor display panels which she usually ignored. They were all showing an ad for InstaSitter, and it didn't take a genius to figure out that the redheaded child shown from behind in the arms of a beatifically smiling Blythe was Dorothy. The rest of the walk home went by with a steaming Kelly on autopilot.

"Where is everybody?" Kelly called as she entered the crew module of the junked ice harvester that the family called home. In their first year of marriage, Joe had put a lot of effort into renovating the utilitarian quarters into

8

something that more closely resembled the interior of a residential suite, but the decks and the bulkheads could only be disguised to a point. On the bright side, it was sized for a large crew to inhabit for extended periods in space, so there was plenty of room for everybody, even when they were all home at the same time. Which was rarely.

Dorothy pulled free from her mother's hand at the sound of a heavy tail thwacking the deck and ran to greet Beowulf, who deigned to roll on his back for the little girl. The giant junkyard dog was well past his prime, and with the advent of Joe's homebrewing hobby/business, had begun to sport a beer belly. But when he felt like standing up and growling, Beowulf could still intimidate anybody who wasn't wearing an armored space suit.

"You can come out of hiding now," Kelly said, employing a conversational tone to show that she wasn't taken in for a minute by the prank. "That's very funny, pretending not to be home for our first family night, but it's getting old."

The only answer was the increased frequency of thumping produced by Beowulf's tail as the little girl began to rub his belly with both hands. Kelly was about to tell Dorothy not to spoil the dog, when she noticed that Beowulf was also trying to catch her eye while pointing at something with his nose, his preferred method of communication. It only took Kelly a few seconds to figure out he was indicating the message board by the front door.

Kelly strained to decipher Joe's lazy scrawl on the touch screen, but she finally worked out the message, "Emergency tow, took Paul to help, don't wait up." Below it, written in Laurel's careful printing, "Called back for night shift. Pays double-time!!!" The last message was in Donna's neat

9

script, "Stopped in with Stan, nobody home. P.S. I think your scary watchdog was having a bad dream."

Two

Joe watched out of the corner of his eye as Paul maneuvered the Nova alongside the alien vessel and began looking for a towing hitch. Paul had insisted on purchasing the Nova with part of the winnings from his championship prize in the Drazen gaming tourney a year earlier, just a few weeks after he turned seventeen. Joe might have refused the gift of a new tug from his foster son as being too generous, if not for the fact that Paul had been telling Joe for four years that he would buy a new ship for Mac's Bones with his winnings.

The alien ship on the main viewing screen looked like nothing either of them had ever seen before, and Joe was beginning to wonder if it even had its own propulsion system.

"It looks like a spherical terrarium with some sort of tree growing out from the center and a weird propeller sticking off the back into space. But what's the propeller supposed to push against?" Paul asked.

"Maybe the propeller is on the front and it's supposed to pull on something," Joe replied for the sake of saying something, since he was just as much in the dark as Paul. "Try the ship-to-ship comm again. Maybe that Dring guy can tell us where to grapple."

As if responding to the mention of Dring's name, the comm came to life by itself, and this time an image of the alien pilot appeared on the main view screen as well. The pilot, who was holding onto a tree branch with his tail, made Joe think of a chubby little dinosaur from a children's cartoon. It had a short snout with the blunt teeth of a herbivore, a pair of dark, saucer-sized eyes, and a crest of brilliant plumage on the top of its head. And it quickly proved itself to be a master of zero gravity yo-yo tricks.

"Ahoy there, Nova. Thank you for responding to my hail. I got your comm address from the ad on the beacon, but you never know how current those things are."

"We're happy to have the business," Joe responded honestly. "Union Station core is so big that most ships either enter under their own power or just get close enough to let the Stryx pull them in with manipulator fields. Has your propulsion system failed?"

"Failed?" The little alien broke into a toothy smile. "No, but I'm not used to maneuvering in such a high traffic area and I thought I'd avail myself of your services. Are you equipped with magnetic grapples?"

"Yes. Just looking for a place to clamp on," Paul answered.

"The end of the spindle is best, on the other side of the rotational mass," Dring informed them.

"Will do," Paul responded, and began maneuvering the tug towards what he had previously termed "the propeller on the back."

"I've never seen a vessel quite like yours before," Joe continued conversationally. "Could you tell us what she is?"

"In a word, obsolete," Dring replied, adding a laugh. "My longtime companion here is a gravity surfer, and the universe never lacks for gravity waves. But the technology is better suited for wandering through the void than moving point-to-point, so it never really caught on. Thinking back, I'm not sure that anyone other than my people ever produced gravity surfers outside of research labs."

"I don't think I've ever come across your people before," Joe continued, as Paul expertly grappled the end of the shaft with magnetic clamps on a guided tow cable. "What I can see of your ecosystem through the hull looks pretty similar to our own ag decks. Are you oxygen/nitrogen breathers?"

"The atmosphere you are maintaining on your tug would suit me just fine," Dring replied. "Speaking of which, I suppose we should agree on a price before you haul me back to the station. I'd be willing to pay extra if you could package the tow with a private docking space, since as you can see, my ship doesn't provide much privacy. Do you know of anywhere I could lay up for a few cycles without attracting too much attention?"

"Grapples connected," Paul announced, and goosed the tug's maneuvering thrusters a few times to wiggle the connected vessels. "Bond is good. We're rigid."

"What do you think about slipping him in behind the old scrap pile?" Joe mused.

"Docking him in Mac's?" Paul moved his hands rapidly within the holo controller field and brought up a three-dimensional scale image of the gravity surfer docked inside the bay which was leased by Mac's Bones. "The living section will be a tight fit, but it should be fine as long as it can stand a couple of bumps. The, uh, rotational mass is going to end up sticking into the scrap pile."

"Don't worry about my dimensions," Dring interjected. "I can reconfigure the hull of the surfer to any shape, and the rotational mass storage position is in line with the spindle. It would take a lot more than a few bumps to do us any damage."

"If you're really planning on staying a couple of cycles, how about five hundred Stryx creds for the tow and three hundred per cycle?" Joe offered.

"That sounds very reasonable," Dring replied. "And I like the sound of being docked behind a scrap pile since I do a bit of metal sculpture when I have the chance. Is it possible I could purchase materials from you?"

The two humans exchanged a humorous glance. "I think we can throw in the sculpture material for free," Joe replied with a grin. "To tell you the truth, our, uh, recycling facility is in a transitional period as we sort of move away from, uh, recycling."

"We're the biggest Raider/Trader barn on the station," Paul added, as he headed the Nova back towards the station.

"I've been out of circulation for a few years," Dring said. "I'm afraid I'm not familiar with this Raider/Trader activity."

"It's the biggest thing in gaming," Paul explained, immediately warming to his subject. "It came out of nowhere last year, though rumor is that it was developed by the Verlocks, because they're the big math heads among the biologicals. The governance module is a set of mathematical algorithms that will run as a training task on just about any ship's control system. But it's integrated with Stryxnet and allows full virtualization of the gameverse on anything the host controller can handle. I've never seen the like for action or realism, and you can make a good living

14

earning in-game currency as a trader, and then selling it for Stryx cred through Bill's Exchange."

"It sounds like you're talking about a game that employs actual ships instead of holograms or virtual consoles," Dring summarized.

"The game allows for real ships, but it's much more than that," Paul enthused. "You start out with a bare-bones ship, minimal propulsion, no weapons and a cargo of low-grade ore, and you have to earn Trader gold to upgrade anything. It all takes place in real-time, meaning an hour of playing is the same as an hour in the real universe, and you can't wave a magic wand and pop out here or there just to find action. If you have a spaceworthy ship, rather than just a control system in a starter-shell or a bedroom mock-up, you can give the governance algo full control and actually fly the same mission as in the gameverse."

"I'm not sure I understand," Dring admitted. "Do you mean you can take an armed ship out in space and fight real battles with other players?"

"The other ships aren't in the same space, and the weapons usually aren't real either, or almost nobody would be able to afford to play. But being out in space means you pull real G-forces in maneuvers, and the propulsion system and weapons have to be maintained and supplied. So when you give the governance algo full control, it sets the upper limit on your capabilities according to the gear you've earned or purchased with Trader gold. But if your real ship exhausts power for weapons or your propulsion system melts down, you're dead in space."

"Tell him about the accidents," Joe prompted sardonically.

"Well, there have been a few idiots who got so caught up in the gameverse that they collided with something in real space or flew into a star, and of course, you don't get to start over after that. And I guess there have been rumors about real weapons discharges causing problems, but you'd have to be a jerk not to employ a safety task to lock out weapons if any real targets come into range," Paul mumbled.

"And what's this 'barn' concept you mentioned?" Dring inquired. "If we'll be sharing the same hold space, I'd like to believe I won't be in any danger."

"Raider/Trader barns are sort of like parking lots for game ships and starter-shells. We have over two hundred players using our hold at this point, but they're all running the game as a training task, of course. Most of the players can't afford spaceworthy ships, and we just sort of stumbled into the business, since there was a huge rush for salvaged control systems when the game got popular. We'd gotten rid of most of the scrap by that point, so we had plenty of space to rent out for starter-shells or mock-ups, for players whose living situation didn't allow them to dedicate a whole room to setting up a command bridge," Paul explained, with a renewed burst of enthusiasm.

"And we do a good business towing the starter-shells away from the station and back, so the hardcore players can get the weightless practice while they're saving money to finish building out the ship," Joe added.

"Ah, this is becoming confusing," Dring said, blinking rapidly. "Do you make money playing the game or providing shipyard services?"

"As a business, we make money selling starter-shells, equipment upgrades, and helping with modifications," Paul answered. "We also let floor space by the month, plus we rent a couple of maxed-out game ships for players who want the full experience, especially for flying raids or battles. And I make money by playing on my own account and selling Trader gold for Stryx creds through Bill's Exchange, mainly to rich players from other species who don't have the patience to work their way up."

"Do the programmers charge a high price for using the game codes?" Dring asked. "It sounds like an expensive game to run, especially with the data transfer charges from the Stryxnet that you mentioned. Do they charge by time, or sell game items for hard currency?"

"The game makers must have some kind of a deal with the Stryx, because they only charge a few creds a month for using the algos, and that includes permanent storage of your game state. All you need to do is enter your ID on any ship controller running the code and you're off and running where you left off the previous time. The game only takes Trader gold for upgrading capabilities, so I don't know what else they can make money on, unless they have a deal with Bill's."

As the Nova's autopilot adjusted course to line up entry with Union Station core, a thought occurred to Joe and he felt the need to caution their tenant-to-be. "And as long as we're on the subject of the Stryx, Dring, I just want to make sure you understand that we aren't smuggling you onto the station. The Stryx monitor all of the interior and the surrounding space, so if you were trying to slip in under their radar, it's not going to happen."

"I would never try to evade the Stryx," Dring replied with a chuckle. "If you're going to hide, hide in plain sight is my motto. But I must admit I'm intrigued by the game your young co-pilot has so enthusiastically described, and I hope I might persuade him to bring me along as supercargo on one of his missions. The study of complex systems is my personal field of endeavor, and it's been my experience that they often serve more than one purpose."

"You're welcome to fly with me, Dring," Paul extended an invitation. "Some people around here think I spend too much time playing Raider/Trader, but most of the gameverse time is spent traveling from place to place, so I can get my course work done or grab a good night's sleep. You can go days at a time without anything happening, but if you expect to make any Trader gold, you do have to keep up with the markets on Stryxnet."

"It sounds like it could be very educational," Dring observed.

"Like a school for pirates," Joe grumbled.

"Graduate school," Paul corrected him, as the rigidly bonded ships entered the Union Station core and began to spin up to the station's rotational speed. Stryx traffic control handled all of the vessels in the core using field manipulators, which eliminated accidents that might have resulted from anti-collision systems that lacked a common protocol. Once a ship was spinning around the invisible central axis at the same speed as the station, the weight that resulted from angular acceleration would gradually increase as the ship moved outwards to a docking bay.

Joe checked the status of the atmosphere retention field on the bay that housed Mac's Bones before triggering the outer hold section at the edge of the bay to slide open. With help from the autopilot, Paul backed the tandem into the cleared area behind the remaining mound of scrap, which was piled almost to the height of the bay doors. As the hull of the gravity surfer touched the decking, it began to flatten, rather like a water balloon placed on a hard surface. After a few moments, Dring's ship was transformed from a sphere to something more like a rapidly melting snowball, and the flora began a slow-motion shift to adapt to the new version of up-and-down.

"Wow!" Paul breathed, "I've never seen anything like that before!"

"You can retract the grapples now," Dring replied, even as he let go of a moving tree limb with his tail, and dropped onto a pile of soft moss that seemed to hump up below his position on command. "It will take a little time for my ship to settle in, and I should remain with her until equilibrium is achieved. Thank you for the tow and the information. I will take you up on your offer to demonstrate the game as soon as possible."

Three

"I don't understand what you have against trying InstaSitter," Joe reasoned with Kelly, as she worked at arranging her hair. "Now that Laurel is in the paid internship part of her chef training and Paul is running a Raider/Trader squadron when he's not working or studying, we can't expect either of them to be available for babysitting, especially on short notice. Of course, I'd be happy to have Dorothy all to myself while you go to the party."

"It's not a party, it's a diplomatic reception. I don't know why I'm starting to get invitations all of a sudden, but it's part of my job to go to these high-level functions. And it's part of your job to escort me," Kelly concluded, casting an accusatory look at Joe.

"So let me call InstaSitter," Joe argued again. "Chastity would have been in touch by now if she was available, and Paul is taking Blythe to the flower show tonight."

"Does she ever let Paul choose where they're going?" Kelly asked crossly. As much as she loved Donna's girls, she worried that Blythe frequently took advantage of Paul's willingness to let his first girlfriend lead him by the nose.

"You can't really blame Blythe for that," Joe replied. "If she let Paul have his way, they'd spend every date on his

Raider building up Trader gold. Unless you want to bring Dorothy along or let the Stryx keep an eye on her, InstaSitter is the only option at this point. I know they aren't cheap, but this game business is bringing in more money than the junkyard ever did, and now that LoveU is paid-off, we can afford a few luxuries."

Kelly glanced guiltily at the new shoes and handbag sitting on the bed next to the designer suit that had replaced her long-serving cocktail dress at diplomatic functions. One thing about being married to an ex-mercenary was that his old uniforms were always acceptable as formal wear, and he showed no interest in shopping for new clothes. She gave in with a sigh.

"If I call InstaSitter, Libby will answer, and then I'll have to explain again why it's not right to let Metoo babysit for Dorothy," Kelly replied. "For some reason, Libby doesn't understand the difference between being friends and taking care of somebody."

"I wonder why that would be," Joe mumbled with a sideways glance at Kelly, as he requested the station exchange to ping InstaSitter through his implant.

"Welcome to InstaSitter. How may we help you?" Although Joe knew the voice was artificially generated, it sounded like a cross between Blythe and Chastity, with a bit of Donna mixed in for maturity. Years of selling flowers outside of the restaurants and bars of the Little Apple had provided the girls with valuable marketing skills. He had no doubt they had Libby try different voice mixes and carefully track the customer response for each species in order to hone in on the perfect pitch.

"Hi, Libby. Is that you doing the voices? I finally talked Kelly into giving InstaSitter a shot."

"That's great, Joe. But please pretend you don't know me when you call in, or I'll have to treat it as my personal business and I won't be able to charge BlyChas Enterprises the management overhead fee."

"BlyChas Enterprises?" Joe echoed. "I guess the girls really are moving up the food chain. Anyway, we're going to this Grenouthian embassy thing, but you already knew that. Kelly is just starting on her hair, so you can work out when we'll be ready to go."

"Your sitter will be there in forty minutes and the charges will be added to your rent for the cycle. Thank you for choosing InstaSitter," the synthesized voice concluded and closed the connection.

"That was easy enough," Joe reported, receiving a grunt from Kelly in acknowledgement. "I'm going to give Dorothy a bath and get her ready for the sitter."

Five minutes later, a boy in his early teens approached the door of the ice harvester and knocked gingerly on the already open door. Beowulf looked up from his bed, examined the visitor through one eye, and returned to his dreams. The boy was uncertain what to do, but eventually he entered the living room and called out, "Hello? Is anybody home?"

Kelly shouted back, "Just a minute," followed by, "Can you get that, Joe?" But between the running water and the years spent being too close to explosive devices when they went off, her husband didn't hear. So Kelly hastily belted her robe and went out to see who had gotten past the dog.

"Hi, I'm Thomas from InstaSitter," the boy launched into a prepared speech as soon as Kelly entered the room. Then he stared for a moment and asked, "Kelly?"

"Yes, I'm Kelly," she replied. "Aren't you rather early?"

"Don't you remember me?" the boy asked. "I'm Thomas, from your embassy mixer. You made sure I got to my Turing/Ryskoff test on time. I passed," he added proudly.

"Thomas!" Kelly exclaimed in surprise and shock at seeing the time-deficient artificial person in an adolescent body. "You've grown younger!"

"Oh, I can explain that," he said. "When the Stryx recognized my personhood at the gaming tourney challenge, I gained the rights of an artificial intelligence, but I lost the use of the rental body the university had provided. The Stryx immediately offered me a loan through their new AI administration branch, but I didn't want to end up with a huge mortgage, so I took a smaller body. I didn't realize that appearing to be so young would impact my earnings potential," he added ruefully.

"But babysitting for InstaSitter is the best you could do?" Kelly asked.

"Well, I was tired of bussing tables in restaurants, so I talked it over with Gryph, and he thought that spending time working with children wouldn't be a bad education. I've babysat for fifty-two different species so far. In fact, I'm sort of the top employee for InstaSitter because I don't need to sleep or breathe. Things must have been slow tonight since you're actually my first human assignment, which will make it fifty-three species."

"Well, that's great, Thomas. I'm glad to see you doing so well. Let me just finish getting ready and I'll introduce you to our daughter."

"I'm looking forward to that," Thomas replied enthusiastically. "Does she dance?"

Kelly flinched and shouted, "Joe, the sitter's here early," before retreating to the bedroom to finish getting ready. Thomas evinced no particular curiosity in his surroundings, or maybe he was afraid of disturbing Beowulf, because he remained motionless until Joe appeared in his old dress uniform, followed by a scrubbed and night-gowned Dorothy.

"Art-ficial person," Dorothy pronounced happily. "Do you know Metoo?"

"I knew your mother a few years ago, but this is my first time meeting you," Thomas replied.

"Joe McAllister," Joe introduced himself and shook hands with Thomas. "I'm sure you have a great deal of babysitting experience since InstaSitter sent you over."

"Oh, yes," Thomas replied. "I've already told Kelly that they consider me their top employee. Do you have any special instructions?"

"Dorothy's already had supper and her bath," Joe answered. "She can stay up another hour if she doesn't act too tired, but it's in bed by 19:00, even if she says she's not sleepy."

"Got it," Thomas acknowledged, and pulling out a pen, wrote "In bed by 19:00," on the palm of his rather inky left hand. Kelly emerged from the bedroom just as the exchange took place, and watched with approval as Thomas took note of the time.

"I guess we can get going a little early ourselves," Kelly said to Joe. "Come on, Pumpkin. Give Mommy a kiss."

"Up!" Dorothy commanded, and gave her mother a kiss on the nose once she was lifted into position. "Bye, bye."

Ten minutes later, with navigational help from Libby, they arrived at the Grenouthian embassy in a section of the station that neither of them had ever visited. The atmosphere had enough nitrogen and oxygen to support their filter plugs function, but the noticeable hum in his nostrils told Joe that they were working pretty hard.

24

The Grenouthians were an old species, and Joe had spent some time on their home planet years before as a largely ceremonial guard for a minor royal house. They made it clear that while they had great respect for humans as potential cannon fodder, inter-species fraternization was strictly prohibited. Joe had only picked up a dozen words of the low frequency speech that made him think of an outsized goose honking, and all of those words were drill-related. So it came as a surprise when they were greeted at the entry by the Grenouthian ambassador and his consort, who appeared to have been waiting especially for the humans.

"Ambassador," the Grenouthian diplomat boomed in a low register that Kelly felt in her toes, even though her implant translated the speech properly and neutralized the sound waves at her ears. It was obvious that the over-grown bunny-like creature with floppy ears had studied up on Earth customs, since he extended a furry hand to shake. But it was equally clear he had missed out on the fact that the EarthCent ambassador was a woman, because he addressed his salutation and offered the handshake to Joe. Joe shook the creature's paw diplomatically, while attempting to cue the ambassador in on his mistake by making head tilts towards Kelly. The Grenouthian's consort lifted one of the ambassador's furry earflaps and whispered something in a higher register, which Kelly felt in her teeth.

"I'm very sorry," the ambassador continued. "My se-cond consort informs me you may suffer from an injury that makes your head move spasmodically. Do you require medical attention?"

"Uh, I'm fine, Ambassador. But my wife, the EarthCent ambassador, is looking forward to being introduced," Joe replied, hoping he wasn't creating a diplomatic incident. But the bunny just turned smoothly to Kelly and repeated his original greeting as if no mistake had occurred. Which reminded Joe of what he had meant to tell his wife about the Grenouthians. They didn't make mistakes, or rather, they never admitted to them.

"Ambassador," Kelly responded to the greeting in kind, thinking it might be an official formula. But when the Grenouthian stood silently for a number of seconds, holding her hand in his warm paw and gazing at her with his bulging bunny eyes, Kelly decided she had better carry the conversation forward. "Thank you for the invitation to your embassy. It came as a bit of a surprise to me, since we've never established relations, and I was unable to even get a response from your government about a human ship that went missing in your space. But it's a lovely reception, and I hope we get the chance to see you and your consort again in the near future."

"Are you leaving?" the ambassador boomed anxiously, tightening his grip on her hand. "But you are our guest of honor. I assure you that we are ready to establish full relations with your EarthCent at any time, and I extend my apologies about the human ship which was destroyed in our space, although I don't have any information about that," he added hastily. "Please, come in and mingle. There are many Grenouthian businessmen present who are waiting to meet you."

Kelly was so taken aback by the Grenouthian's offer of full relations and business ties that she literally didn't know what to say. But her fingers were beginning to go numb from the giant bunny's iron grip, and she was having a hard time looking dignified while he was tugging on her hand. She replied diplomatically, "Since you've offered full relations and help with the missing ship, we'll be happy to stay and talk with your businessmen. If you just let go of my hand, I'll head right in."

"Allow me to introduce you around," the ambassador offered, easing his grip on her hand, but guiding it to his forearm as he stepped closer. Kelly suddenly realized that the ambassador was naked, other than a blue sash running across his chest from one shoulder to the other hip, which was probably his badge of office. But his fur was so incredibly soft and fine that she had to fight the urge to start stroking his arm as she walked with him into the hall. She threw a helpless look over her shoulder at Joe, but he just shrugged and followed a few steps behind, scanning the room for something that looked drinkable.

As the crowd of big furry creatures resolved into individual shapes, some wearing various colored sashes, others in nothing but their fur, Kelly realized two things. First, she and Joe were the only non-Grenouthians present. Second, every last one of the Grenouthians was looking at her anxiously. She blushed.

"Allow me to introduce you to our economic minister," the Grenouthian ambassador boomed as he guided her up to a dark-furred bunny with a gold sash.

"I'm Kelly Frank McAllister," Kelly introduced herself, gingerly offering a hand. "And you are?"

"I am the Economic Minister," the Grenouthian replied, and took a quick slap at her hand. "We would like very much to purchase the proper credentials to send an economic delegation to your Earth. Could you tell me the price please?" The whole room fell silent in anticipation of Kelly's reply.

"We don't charge visiting businessmen for credentials," Kelly told the minister, puzzling over the fact that he had withheld his name, though come to think of it, the ambassador had done the same. "Just contact my office during working hours and we'll set you up."

The economic minister stared at her unblinking for a moment, shook his head, and muttered something under his breath to the ambassador. Thanks to the lack of interference from other conversations and the low frequency sound waves, her diplomatic grade implant picked up the whisper and translated it as: "There's a sucker born every minute." Kelly tried to take comfort in the fact that idioms often translated inaccurately, but it was hard to think of how a positive comment could have been rendered that poorly.

The room came back alive with a bedlam of humming and honking, and Kelly found herself drowning in a sea of close-talking Grenouthians, all requesting credentials to visit Earth on business. She kept repeating the same instructions she had given the economic minister but they all seemed to want to hear it directly from her mouth. Just as she was beginning to get dizzy, she felt Joe pressing something cold into her overheated hand. It was an open bottle of chilled champagne.

"Go ahead and have a swallow," he leaned in and spoke in her ear. "They only had the one bottle and it's obviously intended for us, or for you."

"I can't take much more of this," she complained, shaking an insistent paw off her shoulder and struggling to face her husband in the crush of warm bodies. Joe's eyes were pink and runny, and his face looked a bit bloated as well. "What's wrong? You look terrible."

"Allergies," Joe replied, wiping his runny eyes on the sleeve of his dress uniform. "It's why I only lasted one tour on the Grenouthian home world, even when I loaded up

28

with antihistamines. It's the pollen from their shrubbery that gets into their fur. They must have a warren here on one of their ag decks."

"I'm so sorry," Kelly sympathized, and struggled to stay close to Joe in the milling mass of fur. "Do you want to leave or wait outside?"

"I'll be fine," Joe replied. "I'll bet you haven't noticed, but every Grenouthian you talk to leaves immediately afterwards. Another fifteen minutes and you'll have the place emptied out. Just hang in there and we'll be on our way home before you know it." Joe was elbowed out of the way by a particularly aggressive bunny as he concluded, and Kelly had to restrain herself from taking a swing at the rude creature's prominent buck teeth with the champagne bottle. Instead, she took a long swallow directly from the bottle and turned back to the cuddly mob.

"Yes, you can all have credentials. Just contact my office in the morning. Yes, everybody includes you," she told the next Grenouthian. But they all insisted on addressing her one by one, slapping or crushing her free hand with a paw in an imitation of the human custom. It wasn't until a towering Grenouthian, who spoke to her over the shoulder of a shorter compatriot, kept reaching for her hand and shouting "Contract!" that she realized that the bunnies believed a handshake was necessary to seal her commitment.

After that, the room emptied rapidly as Kelly gave up all attempts at actually speaking with the Grenouthians, beyond offering credentials and shaking hands. When the last bunny left without so much as a "Goodbye," Kelly found herself alone with Joe in the embassy's reception hall. An empty champagne bottle dangled from her hand, and she felt pretty woozy.

"What could all of that have been about?" she asked Joe, feeling like she had been run over by an Easter parade.

"Let's just get out of here," Joe replied with a shrug. "I need a shower, and I don't want to get nose burn to go with my eyes. Haven't you noticed that the filters are working pretty hard?"

"Oh, I thought the humming was from my translation implant. Yes, let's get out of here before they send in another batch," she said, recoiling at the mental image. The two humans rapidly made their way from the embassy to the nearest tube.

Kelly resisted pushing Joe for his thoughts about the weird reception because he looked so miserable and puffy, but he caught her look of pity and managed a smile.

"I look a lot worse than I feel," he told her with a wry grin. "I should have taken a pill. It just didn't occur to me that the room would be so full of fur. I thought it would be your typical Noah's Ark type thing, with just a couple Grenouthians as hosts."

"I don't understand," Kelly mused. "I've only met a few Grenouthians in the seven years I've been here, and none of them would even speak to me. Why would they all be in such a hurry to make nice and visit Earth? How will this affect their relations with the rest of the Natural League?"

"They're an old species, but they're known for being quick on their feet," Joe told her. "They aren't aggressive in the military sense, but they operate a large merchant fleet which specializes in getting in and out of new places before the competition heats up. Maybe they've simply decided that Earth has something worth exploiting."

"But why all of a sudden?" Kelly asked, as the tube capsule smoothly shifted to a different vector, which was only detectable by the change in acceleration. "Other than somebody throwing a giant asteroid at Earth, I can't think of any radical changes since the Stryx restructured the tunnel fees five years ago to give our manufacturers a chance."

"Then there must be something we're missing," Joe assured her. "We're still the new kids on the block. All of these other species were kicking around the galaxy long before our ancestors mastered sailing ships. They may look funny, and sometimes they may act funny, but they're all experts of a sort at inter-species relations or they wouldn't be here."

The champagne she had quaffed over the last twenty minutes had crept up on Kelly. She found herself holding Joe's arm for balance as the capsule began a series of course changes that announced their arrival back in the human section of the station. Finally, the door slid open on the inner docking deck just a short walk from Mac's Bones, and in another minute, they were home.

Thomas and Dorothy were out in front of the ice harvester playing fetch with Beowulf. Dorothy was changed out of her nightgown into her regular jumpsuit.

"What's going on, Thomas?" Kelly demanded. "It's almost an hour past her bedtime!"

"I put her to bed at 19:00, as instructed," Thomas replied with a hurt expression.

"I woke up," Dorothy declared. "Thomas dress'ded me and make breakfast."

Joe started to say something, but Kelly interrupted before he could finish a word. "Thank you, Thomas. I hope she behaved well for you."

"You're welcome, Kelly. I enjoyed babysitting for your daughter. I hope I didn't do anything wrong," he added anxiously.

"No, no. We just didn't give you very good instructions. Tell me, Thomas. Do alien children always sleep through the night?"

"They sleep as long as their parents tell them to sleep," Thomas replied. "They do everything their parents tell them to do. Doesn't it work that way with humans?"

Joe felt so bad about having to push the babysitter out the door that he stuffed a few extra creds into the artificial person's hand. It was necessary because Kelly couldn't stop herself from laughing hysterically every time she looked at Thomas, and Joe was beginning to worry that she would hurt herself.

Four

Paul and Blythe sat side by side on the bridge of his Raider/Trader mock-up, and Dring, after insisting that he didn't require a chair, stood a little behind and between them. Paul would have preferred to take one of the maxed-out rentals into space to give Dring a show, but Blythe always became queasy in weightless conditions. Since they were on a straightforward trading mission with a virtual cargo, being in space wouldn't have added anything other than misery to the experience.

Thrilled to have an intelligent and attentive audience, Blythe took her time explaining the mission to Dring in great detail.

"The first thing I noticed when Paul taught me the game was that the trading algorithm has some weak spots. While it does an incredibly realistic job on the value side, whether you barter or sell for hard currency, it doesn't account for all of the factors that go into cargo storage."

"Do you mean it ignores the mass or the dimensions of the cargo?" Dring asked.

"Nothing that obvious," Blythe replied. "And they do a good job syncing gameverse time to real time. So you can't, say, take on a load of horses and plan to deliver them alive a week later, unless you provide for food and water as well."

"I see." Dring appeared to be giving it serious consideration and stroked his chin in thought. "But perhaps these virtual horses don't complain about the weightless conditions or refuse to load into the hold together?"

"Exactly," Blythe spoke approvingly. "And nobody has to muck out the hold every day either."

"So do you find interstellar horse-trading profitable?"

"Oh no!" Blythe choked down a laugh. "Horses are a money pit. Maybe Joe would find horse-trading interesting since he used to ride them, but there's no profit in it. I was just using horses as an example."

"Ah. When Paul told me we were on Earth approach, I thought animals might be your cargo, since large manufacturers would be unlikely to employ small independent traders."

"That's another weak point in the algorithms," Paul said, drawing a hurt look from Blythe, who was inclined to treat their guest as her personal property. "They allow us to do virtual trades in the gameverse that the guilds or long-term contracts would keep us out of in the real world."

"That's just to make the game interesting," Blythe said "The point I was trying to make is that there are loopholes where the idealized conditions let us make a bigger profit faster than if we were doing the same thing in the real world. Here, just listen," she concluded. The main viewer showed them emerging from the Stryx tunnel back into regular space, practically in Earth's orbit.

"EarthCent control to vessel with transponder code XRTGQ. Please identify yourselves. Over."

"This is the independent trader Blythe," Paul announced, with a self-conscious glance at his passenger to see if he reacted to the ship's name. "We are scheduled to pick up a load of Strontium 90 at Elevator Two. We will not be entering Earth atmosphere. Over."

"Roger that, Blythe," the virtual EarthCent controller responded. "You show on our schedule and ID checks positive. Proceed to Elevator Two for docking instructions."

"Wilco and Out," Paul replied, closing the channel and setting course to intercept Elevator Two. The docking point was a massive anchor satellite on a tether that stretched all the way to a cargo transfer station on Earth's surface. A pair of elevators built under contract by an alien construction consortium had cut the cost of transferring cargo from Earth's surface to orbit by a factor of a thousand.

"Strontium 90," Dring repeated. "My knowledge of human biology is somewhat sketchy, but isn't that a very dangerous substance for you to be transporting?"

"If it was real, I wouldn't get anywhere near it," Blythe responded with a happy grin. "But as virtual cargo, we can carry it in the hold for almost a week without even losing space to virtual shielding. Longer than that, the algorithm would declare us dead, but by that time we'll have sold it to the Frunge, and the game doesn't track long-term radiation exposure to crew. The profits are so good that we could eventually get rich doing this run for Trader gold and exchanging for Stryx creds through Bill's."

"But it would get pretty dull," Paul added. "It only works when we put in the onboard mission time the full turn takes, three days out, five days to the Frunge outpost on Dalen, and another two days back to Union. The last turn took the two of us almost three months of real time to string the hours together."

"But the two of you are a mating pair, so the time must pass quickly," Dring observed.

Paul blushed bright red and mumbled something about just being friends. Blythe shot him a look, and then replied icily, "If this wasn't a great place to catch up on work without distractions, you couldn't get me to lock myself up in this tin can for ten minutes."

"So how do you manage the loading of such dangerous cargo?" Dring asked, changing the subject when he realized he had made them uncomfortable.

"That's the other great thing about it," Blythe replied, perking up instantly. "Because it gets special treatment on both ends of the run, it's all handled by mechanicals, the virtualizations of dumb robots. Paul has to supervise pretty closely to get the packing right, but it's all done without leaving the room."

"It would be too dull for you to just stand and watch, Dring," Paul said. "I'm going to pause the game and Blythe and I will finish up later when we both bring work to do. I was hoping that you could show us around your ship."

"Paul told me about it, and I'd really love to see your garden, Dring," Blythe added.

"Then come along and I'll be happy to give you a tour," Dring answered. The three of them exited the mock-up, finding themselves in the middle of a collection of similar mock-ups and shells arranged in neat rows in Mac's Bones.

"It still makes me feel funny, stepping out of the gameverse and finding myself back here," Paul commented. "But the mock-up isn't nearly as immersive as taking a ship into space. Maybe someday everybody in my Raider squadron will have real ships, but for now we fly all of our missions without ever leaving the barn," he continued wistfully. "You're welcome to come for our next battle, if you like."

"I'd appreciate that opportunity very much," Dring replied. Then he led the group towards the long mound of scrap that most visitors to Mac's Bones thought was piled against the side wall of the cavernous hold. Dring guided them confidently to what appeared to be a shallow indent in the mound, but which proved to be the entrance to a tunnel that took a ninety-degree-turn almost immediately. After a few steps to the left, the tunnel turned back again and took a beeline to the other side, where the gravity wave surfer was parked.

"Joe lent me some torches to do sculpture work, so I asked for permission to create this passage," Dring explained. "It was a good way to get practice with his tools."

Paul's mouth dropped open as far as Blythe's when they emerged before the ship. It was completely transformed, now appearing as a long, narrow greenhouse with a fantastical garden and a grove of trees grouped around a small pond, all swarming with little creatures of different types. The transparent hull was only noticeable due to subtle rolling distortions and interference patterns, as if it were made from a liquid into which somebody was continually tossing pebbles.

"My ship is quite flexible, as you can see, and my traveling companions enjoy being back on solid ground, even if the feeling of gravity is just from the station's spin."

"Where were all of these little creatures when we met your ship in space?" Paul asked. "And what happened to the big central tree thing?"

"My little friends prefer to hibernate in their burrows when we're in space and there's no up or down," Dring explained. "When the ship takes its spherical form, the water is cradled in the center surrounded by what you saw as a tree, which extends its limbs in all directions and provides hollows for those who prefer to be inside. We can survive for quite a long time as a closed system, and losses are easily made up from the elements drifting through space."

"Can we go inside?" Blythe asked, her eyes devouring the flora. "I spent a few years in the flower business and I've never seen plants like yours."

"By all means, enter," Dring invited them with an elaborate bow, and a door-sized section of the hull became perfectly clear, making the hypnotic ripples of the surrounding sections more solid by contrast. Blythe stepped forward, testing for a surface with her fingers, as if checking for the location of a wall in the dark. Then she moved confidently inside, followed by Paul and Dring.

A flock of bird-like creatures with preternaturally intelligent eyes swirled around them, with a few of the more ambitious members finding perches on their shoulders. All of the little creatures were quite vocal about the surprise visitors, creating a chorus of tweets and whistles that the translation implants allowed to pass without interpretation.

"My friends are pleased to make your acquaintance." Dring spoke with a certain formality as the creatures fell silent. Paul suspected he was passing on a message, rather than just being polite.

"Please tell them we are happy you chose to dock in our bay," Paul answered, curious to see if there would be a response. Sure enough, Dring whistled and trilled as hundreds of little heads cocked to listen, after which there was a positive cacophony of responses.

"Enough, enough," Dring said in English, then whistled some more, while making a scattering motion with his hands. The flock dispersed to their favorite nooks and crannies, allowing Dring to lead the young couple to the central pond. Floating plants of different types colonized the surface of the water, and some colorful things that Blythe would later describe as not-quite-fish flashed about below.

"Your ship is just stunning, Dring." Blythe spoke with a deep admiration that she reserved for special occasions. "I've been to immersives that featured human colony ships with self-contained ecosystems that are a thousand times larger than yours, but somehow, there's something unnatural about them. Everything here seems to be in perfect harmony. I'd swear I was standing on the surface of a planet."

"Don't look up," Dring warned her with a gentle chuckle. "The bay doors have a way of destroying the illusion."

"It really is impressive, Dring. Other than you and the tree limbs, I don't recognize anything from the ship we towed in a few weeks ago," Paul added.

"We have had a lot of practice shifting things about, my friends and I," Dring said modestly. "To be honest, I was trying for an environment that humans would be comfortable in, based on what I've seen of your entertainments transmitted over the Stryxnet. If the two of you were actors in a drama, this is the part where you'd take young Blythe in your arms and declare that you've found the Garden of Eden. What did humans do in this Garden of Eden that made it so desirable?"

Paul kicked at the ground and stammered out something unintelligible, but Blythe came to his rescue, saying, "It's a basic human characteristic to desire to be places where we aren't wanted. Humans in dramas want to return to the Garden of Eden because we got kicked out."

"Indeed," Dring mused. "Well, you are welcome here any time during my stay. It certainly makes more sense than letting your desires lead you to trespass elsewhere. Some species aren't very forgiving."

Five

"There must be over a hundred invitations here!" Kelly exclaimed to no one in particular. She scrolled around the collage of colorful messages that had been waiting on her display desk when she arrived at the embassy Monday morning. In each instance, touching the message brought it front-and-center at its optimum size, along with the English translation. Putting aside cultural differences in the style and formality of the diplomatic language, they all started pretty much the same way:

"The (fill in the blank) embassy requests your presence at a special reception to be held this (fill in the blank) evening."

From there, the texts diverged, depending on how the aliens viewed themselves in the galactic pecking order. Invitations from the newer or less aggressive species ended with a simple RSVP, while those who felt themselves to be speaking from a position of strength concluded with horrifyingly detailed threats should Kelly refuse the invitation for any reason.

Strangest of all, Kelly couldn't help noticing that the threats weren't just directed at humans, but at other aliens as well. The invitation from the Frunge, for example, was primarily a rant against the Drazens, and a warning to the humans not to be taken in by Drazen schemes. The Verlock invitation, more properly described as a directive, implied that Kelly was at the head of a multi-species conspiracy to rob the Verlocks of their rightful place in the galaxy. Even the ambassador for the normally friendly Drazens, the only Natural League member that officially recognized Earth, included a warning not to get involved with double-dealing Dollnicks.

Kelly clenched her fists, threw back her head, and yelled, "Libbbbbby!" Releasing the energy immediately made her feel better, though it also brought Donna charging into the room from the outer office.

"Is something wrong, Mrs. Ambassador?" Libby inquired innocently over the room speakers.

Seeing that Kelly was looking a bit sheepish about her outburst, Donna was about to turn around and leave, but Kelly motioned her to stay.

"Official meeting for the EarthCent embassy on Union Station," Kelly announced with a show of professional calm. "Ambassador Kelly McAllister and embassy manager Donna Doogal in attendance. Stryx station librarian is requested to record and participate. Libby, what on Earth is going on?"

"I take it this is in regard to your sudden popularity?" Libby asked insincerely. "I seem to recall somebody complaining not so long ago that EarthCent was making no headway in establishing relations with the elder species."

"But I've never even heard of more than half of these species! And if it wasn't for the gaming tournament we co-sponsor with the Fight On consortium every year, I'd only recognize most of those aliens from crashing parties."

"I always told you that Stan's work was important," Donna interjected, seizing the opportunity to defend her husband's career as the lead information trader for the

Fight On gaming guild in the sector. "Anyway, it was obvious something strange was going on when that flood of Grenouthian requests for trading credentials came in a couple weeks ago. Whatever it is, it looks like word got out."

"Well, I can't take another evening of shaking paws with giant bunnies who can't even be bothered to introduce themselves," Kelly declared for the record. "Is it going to be the same with all of these receptions? And I couldn't attend them all if I wanted to because half of them are scheduled for this coming Saturday night!"

"Please direct your attention to the display desk," Libby instructed the women. The overlapping invitations had been replaced by a diagram showing thousands of worlds with dense patterns of colored lines running between them. "This representation shows Earth's integration into the galactic economy as measured by the flow of Stryx creds, which we track very closely through quantum tagging. For comparison, I've started with how things looked six years ago."

"So all of the blue lines represent Stryx creds flowing into Earth, and the red lines are Stryx creds leaving?" Donna hazarded a guess.

"Yes. Practically all of the inflow of Stryx creds was accounted for by remittances from human migrant laborers employed around the galaxy. The red lines show the same funds leaving to pay for imported goods, and the yellow lines, of which there aren't many, show the income from Earth exports. But the picture changed dramatically after we began the profit-sharing arrangement on Earth cargoes using our tunnel network. Next slide," Libby intoned in a professorial voice, bringing laughs from her audience.

"Close to balanced," Kelly remarked, as the combined blue and yellow lines looked about even with the red. "And the overall flow looks at least double of what it was before."

"That's a good guess," Libby confirmed Kelly's estimate. "The magnitude of emigrant remittances to Earth has remained fairly steady as humans put down roots in their new homes and spend their increased income locally. But the value of Earth exports has grown so quickly that it's caught up with the remittance income, putting Earth on a sound financial basis. This was the picture just a year ago. Next slide."

"What happened?" Kelly exclaimed, looking at the mass of white lines that had practically swamped the blue and the yellow on the map, and even outweighed the swollen red lines by a healthy margin.

"This image shows an average of the daily flows over the last month," Libby explained. "The white lines represent uncategorized inflows of Stryx creds to Earth, and while they were depicted on the previous images as well, the lines were so thin that you couldn't see them."

"Is that like smuggling income or money laundering?" Donna asked.

"We don't really classify any trade as smuggling since we have no laws against it. The same is true for money laundering, as all Stryx creds are created equal. The uncategorized flows are simply monies that are unaccounted for by our register system, so they could be transferred to Earth as hard currency, or using the monetary backbone of another species. Moving beyond total reliance on the Stryx register system is part of the normal evolution of worlds we have fostered, but the amount of currency involved in this case is extraordinary. Looking at

Earth exclusively from the standpoint of cash flow, you've jumped from the level of a slowly developing and somewhat backward planet, to the level of some of the poorer members of the Natural League."

"So now everybody and his uncle are interested in doing business with us," Kelly concluded with an incisive leap of logic. "That explains the furry businessmen and the rush of invitations, but where is the money coming from?"

"I don't know," Libby answered honestly. Donna shot Kelly with a rare look of respect for having figured out the puzzle so quickly. "The Stryx register system protects the integrity of our currency and allows for large transfers using our network and programmable coins, but we specifically designed Stryx creds so that they can also be used in parallel systems. We track the locations and the amounts of all creds in circulation, hiding them from us would mean destroying the value. But we don't attempt to violate the privacy of users and determine ownership."

"So you know the money is real, but that's about it," Donna ventured, to clarify the situation in her own mind.

"Yes," Libby replied. "Since Jeeves has become the Stryx expert on humans, I've been consulting with him in recent weeks as to what it could all mean. But there doesn't appear to be anything amiss, other than the fact that some people on Earth are amassing a great deal of wealth."

"So we know why I'm getting all of these invitations, but how am I supposed to represent Earth at more than fifty different receptions at the same time this Saturday?" Kelly asked, rubbing her temples in frustration.

"Make them come to us," Donna suggested. "I can rent a room at the Empire Convention Center, and we can bring in some friends and family to mill around. It beats having them turning up here, and finding out the whole embassy consists of two middle-aged women in a couple of rented rooms with some part-time help."

"Libby? Will they accept our invitations?" Kelly asked.

"It's an excellent idea, and they won't have much choice other than to accept. I would suggest bringing along a stack of official-looking certificates to hand out if they ask for trading credentials. I've just checked the scheduling for the available rooms at the Empire, and their best-equipped room for a mix of species is available a week from Friday."

"Book it," Kelly said decisively. "I'll start cramming my alien identification holo pack so I'll have a clue who's who, and Donna can handle all of the catering arrangements. We better take the room for a whole day, and—hey, I've got an idea. Why don't we invite some of the Earth merchants on the station to come and set up booths and treat it like a little Earth Exposition?"

"I love it," Donna said, as soon as she stopped laughing. "The last time we tried an Earth Exposition, nobody showed up, and we all ate leftover finger sandwiches for a week. This time we'll have a captive audience."

"I'd like to accept the Drazen invitation if you think they can keep it confidential, Libby," Kelly added on reflection. "They're the only Natural League species that ignored the Earth boycott, and they've helped out quietly here and there over the years."

"I'll contact the Drazen ambassador myself and make the conditions clear. Their invitation is for this Saturday night. I'll respond to the rest through the EarthCent system to save you both time and to give your guests the maximum notice."

"Thanks, Libby, you're a lifesaver. I was afraid Kelly was going to dump all of the correspondence in my lap." Donna sounded genuinely relieved, as her previous experiences with sending diplomatic invitations to other ambassadors involved wasting lots of time on composing formal language for aliens who didn't bother to RSVP.

"Meeting adjourned," Kelly declared. To prove her good intentions, she immediately brought up her alien identification holographic series that matched names with home worlds.

From the outer office, Donna could hear Kelly reciting, "Hoong. Next. Uh, uh, uh, Mengoth. Next. I know this. Wait! Strapii. No, I take it back. Wait, don't tell me, Kraaken! Next." Donna got back up from her desk and swiped the control pad of the normally open door to Kelly's inner sanctum. The door slid shut just as Kelly cried out, "Theosomething!"

Twenty minutes later, Donna looked up from her exposition-planning labors to discover a jolly-looking lizard with feathered crest standing before her. Dring said that he knew Paul and Joe and had been told to stop by to visit Kelly at any time. The embassy manager pinged her boss, who was already worn out from looking at holograms of aliens, so Donna swiped the door back open and introduced the pleasantly plump visitor.

"Ambassador Kelly McAllister, this is Dring," Donna announced the guest, before withdrawing to the outer office.

"Dring. Please make yourself at home," Kelly offered. "I'm afraid that none of these chairs would be comfortable for you, but if you give us prior warning in the future, we can always rent something that will be suitable."

"No need at all," Dring declared, offering a warm display of teeth that reminded Kelly of a stuffed dinosaur toy she had slept with as a little girl. "I've heard so much about you from your husband. Did he tell you I was renting space for my ship in your scrap area?"

"So that's what he was talking about," Kelly replied. "Yes, he told me something, but I guess I wasn't really listening because I thought you were just another tenant for their Raider/Trader barn. I hear so many names at home these days that I'm afraid I don't remember any of them. And now I'm on a crash course to confusion," she added with a smile, waving a hand at a hologram of something that looked like a large cucumber with eyes and tentacles.

"Ah, a native of Corithander," Dring identified the hologram. "If you meet one, try to avoid letting it touch you with its appendages unless you see it's dragging a length of copper cable like a tail. They tend to build up large static charges in a low humidity atmosphere if not properly grounded."

"Corithander! I almost had it," Kelly declared, though in truth she had been drawing a complete blank. "And may I ask where you're from, Dring, and if the embassy can be of any service?"

"My people have wandered the stars for so long that we've lost the name of our home world. Some of my peers even claim it's a myth. My own studies indicate that our world suffered some calamity that made it inhospitable and we were forced to flee. But that's based on an analysis of ancient poetry, which only exists in fragmentary form," Dring said apologetically.

"But surely you have a name for yourselves," Kelly pressed the chubby little dinosaur for an answer.

"Human?" Dring responded.

"Yes, I'm human. And you are?" Kelly spoke this last bit slowly, complete with pointing at her own chest and then at his, as if talking to a child.

"Human?" Dring repeated. "I don't know another word in your language to substitute."

"Oh, I understand. It's a translation issue," Kelly said, relieved that she had found a way out of the circular discussion. "Yes, I can see why any alien, I mean, sentient species, would call itself human in English. But my translation implant always renders it into the proper word, I mean, the word I would recognize. Maybe the implant has trouble with your language, though it is the diplomatic grade provided by the Stryx."

"But I'm speaking English," Dring protested. "I hope my pronunciation isn't so bad that it needs to be translated for you."

Kelly sat up straighter in surprise. "You speak English? Who learns English? I've been told that nobody else gets our literature and language arts, and that we just don't make sense, even in translation."

"Your books and your poetry are precisely what I wanted to meet you about. I've been tapping into your entertainment transmissions over the Stryxnet for some time now, that's how I learned your language. I see that many of your best entertainments are based upon a book, but I've never come across a full text being broadcast."

"I can get you whatever you want," Kelly told the self-identified human. "I brought a whole library with me in digital format, and I even have a collection of reprinted paper books you could borrow from, as long as you don't leave Mac's with them," she hastened to add. "I mean, you can take one, and when you return it, you can take another. It's kind of traditional on space stations."

"That's very generous of you. Any system you choose is fine by me. I don't want to take any more of your time while you're working, but if I could stop by the house this evening to access your library and borrow a real book, I'll be in your debt."

He called the ice harvester a house, Kelly mused, after saying goodbye to the friendly creature.

Six

Kelly took the lacquered wood hair pin and stabbed it into the mass of red hair she had piled high on her head, but the whole construction came tumbling down as soon as she moved. "So much for being a fashion model," she muttered darkly at the mirror, and began plaiting a braid she could coil up and pin instead.

The InstaSitter showed up in the living room a few minutes early, so Joe introduced the girl to Dorothy and showed her where to find everything. When Kelly came out of the bedroom, she glanced at her faux-mechanical wristwatch and realized they were going to have to run to be in time for the private Drazen dinner party.

"Come here, my Honeybunch," she called to Dorothy, and gave her a kiss. "Oh, you're so sweet. Could Mommy take just one little bite?"

Dorothy squealed with pretend fear and ran to hide behind the babysitter's legs.

"You're safe until we get home. But then I'm going to eat you right up."

"Eat me right up," Dorothy repeated with glee, as the babysitter looked at Joe uncertainly.

"You take good care of my little midnight snack," Kelly told the alien girl with a wink. "And no parties. We'll be back in four hours at the latest."

"Yes, ma'am," the sitter responded politely, though Kelly thought she looked a little nervous.

"Come on, Kel. I covered everything with Tinka while you were getting ready," Joe told Kelly, and gave her a push towards the door. In Joe's mind, the sooner they left, the sooner they would get home. He had yet to attend an alien diplomatic function that served beer worth drinking, though he did enjoy turning off his translation implant and listening for languages that he knew, or at least, recognized.

"Bye, bye, Sweetie Pie," Kelly said, and moved her jaw in exaggerated chomping motions as Joe dragged her out the door. Dorothy clung to Tinka's legs and shrieked in pleasure.

The EarthCent ambassador and her husband followed the Drazen ambassador's directions to his home, where Libby had suggested they meet unofficially to avoid arousing the jealousy of a hundred other species vying for Earth's newfound wealth. The atmosphere in the Drazen sections of the station was close enough to Earth normal that nose filters weren't required, and Drazens had always made themselves at home in the human entertainment district.

An attractive young woman who turned out to be the ambassador's daughter greeted them at the door. She led them into a modest dining room, where the table was spread with take-out containers from various Little Apple restaurants. It smelled like barbeque, and Joe began to salivate.

"Welcome to our home, honored guests," the Drazen ambassador greeted the human couple. "Allow me to introduce my wife, Shinka, and my daughter, Minka." The three Drazens bowed jauntily, comfortable with their traditional customs but not getting carried away. Kelly introduced Joe to Ambassador Bork, after which their Drazen hostess insisted that eating comes before business. Without further ado, they all sat down at the table and dug in.

"I noticed that your name and your daughter's name sound very similar," Kelly remarked to Shinka between bites of sushi and french fries, a combination she had never encountered in a restaurant. "I recall now that our babysitter's name is Tinka. Is it just a coincidence?"

Shinka looked slightly uncomfortable, as if the question had been inappropriate. Then her eyes lit up and she whistled a little tune. Minka whistled something in harmony, and both women looked quite pleased.

"I believe your translation implant is taking some liberties with our names," she informed Kelly. "All Drazen women call ourselves by a series of musical notes that establish our heritage and family position. If the translation I received back is correct, we were identified to you as being named 'Mother,' and 'Daughter,' which I can assure you are just prefixes. Your babysitter's name was translated, 'Younger Daughter,' which means she has older siblings, but it wouldn't be enough to ask for her in a room with other Drazens. Do you understand?"

"Yes, thank you. I've only met male Drazens to this point and their names seem to be unrelated, so it hadn't come up before."

"Drazen males are named whatever," Shinka explained to Kelly casually. "Just so they know to come when we call them."

The Drazen ambassador choked on the chicken finger he was eating and began slapping himself on the back with his tentacle, but he didn't contradict his wife. Joe slid him a bottle of imported beer from the unexpected six-pack that had been placed on the table like a centerpiece, and the Drazen responded with a head nod. The men continued eating in silence, while the wives, in their newfound intimacy, began comparing notes on teenagers and puberty, at which point Minka made a hasty apology and fled the room.

When the beer was finished, Joe leaned back from the table in deep contentment and began the struggle not to fall asleep. Fortunately, Kelly remembered her diplomatic duties and asked her counterpart what she could do for him.

"I'll get right to the point," the ambassador said. "Somebody on your home world is raking it in, and the local Drazen business community is always looking for new capital infusions. I've told them that you humans aren't at all xenophobic when it comes to business, but they are pushing me to obtain special EarthCent trading credentials for them."

"We're happy to oblige," Kelly told him, and withdrew a sheaf of paper documents, all embossed with the green EarthCent seal. "My, uh, staff thought that these might solve your problem, but we'd appreciate if you can keep it quiet until after our Earth Exposition this coming Friday. Is there anything else?"

Ambassador Bork eagerly flipped through the impressive looking stack of credentials, which were printed on special EarthCent letterhead bond paper originally intended for vaccination certificates.

The original exodus of humans after the Stryx first contact had attracted hordes of unskilled laborers from the poorest countries, a few of whom carried with them the seeds of diseases that had been wiped out in the wealthier nations. Fortunately, a combination of advanced medical technology and spaceport health screening equipment had rendered the vaccination certificates obsolete almost immediately, leaving EarthCent with a mountain of official looking paper that had no practical use. A bright intern had hit on the idea of distributing the paper among the far-flung embassies in order to free up space at the main office.

"These will do very nicely," Bork declared. "Thank you. Now the only item remaining on the agenda is to discuss a military alliance between our peoples."

Joe snapped out of his fast food and beer coma at the ambassador's matter-of-fact declaration, and looked to his wife to see how she would respond. Kelly was utterly floored, and she was trying to decide whether to contact Libby for advice, when the Drazen ambassador's daughter returned to the room. Her tentacle was erect behind her head and twitching erratically, a sure sign of emotional distress, and she whispered urgently to her mother. The ambassador's wife immediately rose to her feet.

"Thank you very much for coming," Shinka announced abruptly. "It was very nice meeting you and I hope you come again. But you really need to be getting home."

Kelly and Joe rose reflexively. The Drazen ambassador fixed his wife with an inquisitive gaze, trying to read her mind, but he said nothing in objection.

"You're very welcome," Kelly offered uncertainly. "Is something wrong?"

"No, no," Shinka insisted as she ushered them rapidly to the door. "You have nothing to worry about now, but you really need to go home. The sooner the better."

On their way to the lift tube, Joe and Kelly speculated about what could possibly have been so important to cause the ambassador's wife to terminate the dinner party in the middle of an unprecedented offer of a military alliance, especially considering that Earth lacked a star fleet. Kelly assumed it was a problem with the daughter, since she had looked so embarrassed when whispering to her mother, but Joe was betting that the girl had relayed urgent instructions from the Drazen home world.

Beowulf was waiting near the entrance of Mac's Bones to greet them when they got home, and if Kelly wasn't mistaken, the dog's face wore an expression that looked like he was anticipating some special amusement. Joe decided to take a walk around the hold to check on the Raider/Trader players and stop by Dring's. Breaking with years of tradition, Beowulf chose to follow Kelly instead of Joe. Kelly's eyes opened wide when she saw Donna and Chastity standing in the door of the ice harvester, but Dorothy was right there behind them, hopping from one foot to the other in excitement.

"What's going on?" Kelly asked. "What happened to the sitter?"

"Tinka want to rescue me," Dorothy reported proudly.

"Sit down, sit down," Donna said, leading Kelly into the living room. "I can't believe you're back so early. Did everything go alright?"

"Yes and no," Kelly replied, studying all the suspiciously grinning faces. The presence of Jeeves without Paul tipped her off that something unusual was afoot, but she decided to carry on as if she hadn't noticed. "It was a diplomatic success, I guess, but something happened and the ambassador's wife basically shooed us out the door all of a sudden. I think she was embarrassed."

"And she didn't say anything about a certain request for asylum?" Donna asked, struggling to choke back her laughter.

"No," Kelly answered sharply, frustrated by the unexpected collection of guests and the undercurrent of mirth in the room. "What's this all about?"

"Eat me up," Dorothy squealed happily, and threw herself at her mother's legs. Kelly almost fell off her heels with the suddenness of the attack, but she quickly recovered, and picking up the squirming girl, turned to Chastity for answers.

"Did something go wrong with the girl you sent?" she demanded from the fifteen-year-old co-owner of InstaSitter.

"The system worked perfectly," Chastity answered with a show of dignity, and then she lapsed back into giggles. "Our sitter reported a case of a parent threatening a child and requested a supervisor to come and take Dorothy into custody."

"That's ridiculous!" Kelly protested. "Joe would never threaten our daughter."

"It wasn't Joe, it was you," Donna couldn't help herself from interjecting. "Apparently, you thought the Drazen girl wouldn't see through your cannibalistic intentions."

"Cannibalistic!" Kelly was stunned.

"Eat me up, eat me up," Dorothy chanted in her ear, and the truth began to dawn on Kelly.

"Tinka was so upset by the time I got here that she wouldn't leave Dorothy in my custody, even though I brought mom along," Chastity explained. "She even called the Drazen embassy to request emergency asylum for Dorothy, but for some reason they turned her down. We

57

had to get Libby to send Jeeves, because Tinka wouldn't leave Dorothy alone with humans. She's very responsible."

Jeeves moved forward and contributed his part to the story. "The babysitter questioned your daughter carefully and recorded the interview through her implant before contacting InstaSitter. Dorothy repeatedly confirmed your intention to eat her. It's really an amusing video," he added dryly, as Dorothy beamed at being the center of so much attention.

"Tinka insisted on filling out an official InstaSitter complaint, even after Jeeves explained your strange behavior to her, so I'm afraid you're on our watch list now. You can still get sitters, but you have to agree to Stryx monitoring. Uh, there's an extra thirty centee per hour surcharge," Chastity wrapped up apologetically.

"Libby watches me!" Dorothy said, nodding happily.

"So all's well that ends well," Donna concluded. Then she gave Dorothy a kiss and spared a look of pity for the stunned speechless ambassador before pushing her own daughter towards the door. "Let's go, Chastity. I think Aunty Kelly has had enough humiliation for the night to keep her diplomatic ego in check for a while. See you at the office."

"I officially release Dorothy into your custody," Jeeves intoned, then zipped out the door before Kelly could put her daughter down and find something to throw at the speedy Stryx. The EarthCent ambassador stood fuming, looking for somebody to take out her frustration on, but despite his knowing grin and lolling tongue, she wisely kept Beowulf off limits for target practice.

It took two bedtime stories to counteract the excitement of the evening enough for Dorothy to fall asleep, by which point Kelly found she had calmed herself as well. Other than looking silly in front of the Drazen ambassador's wife, who had obviously been tipped off to the babysitter's asylum request for Dorothy, there's no harm done, she reflected. Embarrassing cultural misunderstandings were part and parcel of the diplomatic life. But she wasn't too happy about Libby not giving her a heads-up as to what was going on, probably due to Jeeves interfering for the sake of a good show.

"Where did everybody go, Kel?" Joe asked, returning from his stroll around the hold. Kelly immediately realized he was completely in the dark about the cannibalism allegation and decided to try to keep it that way.

"They were just here to pitch a special new program InstaSitter is trying out. For a few centees an hour extra, Libby keeps an eye on the babysitters for us. Isn't that great?" she lied smoothly. It turned out that twenty years of diplomatic service hadn't gone completely to waste after all.

Seven

Laurel banged on the table with a ladle to get the attention of her crew, most of whom were classmates from the all-species culinary college she attended. Her long hair was piled up and hidden beneath a floppy white chef's hat, and she wore a clean white lab coat over her clothes, just to help everybody remember who was in charge. They had already set out twenty-five folding tables with white tablecloths and close to two hundred folding chairs. She was a little nervous as she had never catered a war before, though Paul assured her it was more of a police action.

"They'll be coming out of their ships in twenty minutes, so get those grills cranked up. Dinka and Hort, you make sure there are two full sets of condiments on every table. I'll be working the main line with Zella, and Tosh is going to handle the deep fryer. We've done this before, people. There are just more of them today. Oh, and don't start feeding the dog or he'll never leave you alone," she concluded, pointing her ladle at Beowulf.

Beowulf gave her an injured look and began vigorously scratching an ear, part of his "I'm just a poor dog in a cruel galaxy" act. But from his vantage point in the doorway of the ice harvester, he had an excellent view of the five-by-five grid of tables, and was just waiting for the hungry gamers to emerge from their ships. If the rush for food and a seat didn't result in a few players dropping their overloaded plates, it would be child's play for the retired war dog to arrange for an accident.

Inside the command vessel, Paul was leading his squadron to their seventh straight victory, this time over a combined fleet of Frunge and Horten privateers. Some of the players in the Frunge fleet were operating out of another barn on the station, but the Horten gamers were an elite group of wealthy young men who were actually maneuvering their vessels and firing their weapons in a designated game zone in Horten space. The actions of the different forces were all virtualized and communicated through the ship controllers in real-time over the Stryxnet, which employed some eerie quantum-coupling technology that only the Stryx had mastered.

Dring stood behind Paul and his co-pilot, a gangly young man who worked for the Fight On guild and answered to the name "Patches," though nobody could remember why. Paul handled both the piloting and the coordination of squadron maneuvers, while Patches was responsible for fire control and active countermeasures. The two young men were clearly running on adrenaline, with Paul exerting every ounce of concentration he had acquired on the path to becoming Nova grandmaster.

"Alpha-Beta-Gamma," Paul announced the end of the action to his squadron over the encrypted comm channel. There were some groans of protest in return, but signing onto a squadron for a share of the glory also meant accepting the authority of the squadron leader. The two fleets separated in virtual space, and the Frunge backed off rapidly in acceptance of the disengagement. Isolated Horten vessels continued making feints and launching their remaining ordnance, as if returning to their barn with a torpedo unfired could open them up to an accusation of stinginess.

"You run a well-disciplined group," Dring complimented the young commander. "I didn't give you much of a chance against the superior forces you faced, but your opponent's actions were poorly coordinated. I'm not an expert on military maneuvers, but it appeared to me that many of their pilots were pursuing individual glory at the expense of their comrades."

"Yeah, they suck," Patches summed up the action succinctly. "Some of the Frunge aren't bad, but those Hortens are a bunch of rich kids who pilot real hot ships and buy all of their gameverse enhancements with Trader gold purchased on the exchange. It's the training time we put in without ever leaving the barn that counts. The Horten concept of training is flying around an asteroid belt vaporizing rocks with real weapons and sending a live video feed to their girlfriends."

"It's their lack of clock management that really hurts them," Paul added, to soften his co-pilot's assessment of their adversaries. "It's not like we're out in space fighting to the last man, nobody has unlimited time to spend playing. They challenged us to a thousand-tick round, a little under six hours in our time, and it's up in another ten minutes. The encapsulation strategy they were employing might have beaten us in the end if we were out here for three days, but you have to play to the circumstances. They just don't get that we're fighting for points, and there's not a lot you can do when time starts running down."

Dring stroked his chin and thought for a moment. "I'm still a little unclear as to the purpose that fighting serves in the greater game. If I understand you correctly, a raid on a colony or commercial shipping allows you to take the spoils of war, but what do you achieve by meeting other ships in space for large-scale conflicts that would only seem to drain your respective resources?"

Patches blinked at Dring in surprise, as if the victory spoke for itself, but Paul supplied the technical answer. "The game requires an hour of combat for every ten hours in the gameverse to maintain your player profile, whether you want to fight or not. Raids made for spoils don't count. It has to be combat against a numerically competitive foe, no more than a fifty-percent difference in the number of ships or a twenty-percent difference in the average enhancement level of the equipment."

Dring slapped his tail on the deck with glee and favored Paul with a wide, toothy, smile. "This game becomes a better example of a complex system with every new rule I learn. Is there a compelling reason for you to fight in fleets rather than going off on your own?"

"At first a lot of players preferred to seek out one-on-one duels. But it became apparent pretty quickly that the rich kids who were buying all the in-game enhancements would usually win the single combats, simply because they always had twenty percent more firepower. And if you lose a single combat and get vaporized, you have to start building your gameverse ship over again from scratch. But when you participate in a fleet action with a time limit, the right strategy and execution can even the odds against a superior force. And your buddies can usually shield you from being completely destroyed, so you only lose what you're spending on energy."

"Time," Patches announced, and unlocked the hatch of the ship. All around them the hatches were popping open on shells and mock-ups, and excited young men were descending ramps or ladders. The contrast between the virtual battlefield and the catered picnic was jarring, but the victorious players had worked up a serious appetite. They quickly mobbed the cook line Laurel had set up between the Raider/Trader barn and the folding tables.

Mixed in with the boisterous crowd of young males was a solo female crew, consisting of Chastity and Tinka. They had been mutually impressed with each other's character in the aftermath of what the Drazen community referred to as "The Dorothy Incident." When Chastity learned that Tinka was also a Raider/Trader player, she had easily talked her into joining Paul's squadron for their first fleet battle. Tinka had tried to join a barn in the Drazen section, but the males, who were subject to rule by the traditional matriarchy at home, were having no part of it.

"Laurel's a great cook, but this is just quick stuff to feed a bunch of young guys who don't even know what they're eating," Chastity told her new friend. "I assume you like human food because we used to see Drazen couples eating out in the Little Apple all the time. But we never figured out why they didn't buy any flowers from us."

"Drazens are very sensitive to odors, especially dating couples," Tinka explained. "Your ripe flowers—no, that's not the word—your flowers that are in bloom are quite overpowering. They would mask the subtle scents that tell us about compatibility. If you wanted a product to sell dating Drazens, a decongestant would do much better."

"So have you eaten human grill meat before?" Chastity asked, then she put her hand over her mouth when she realized what Tinka's translation implant was likely to make of the question. "Oh, you know what I meant, right?"

"I've had your chicken, or at least the friend who took me to the restaurant told me it tasted like chicken. It reminded me of Drazen snake, to tell you the truth."

"Well, in addition to chicken they're grilling hamburgers and hotdogs. It's pretty much the traditional picnic, along with potato salad, macaroni salad, and green salad. Plus mounds and mounds of french fries," Chastity added, running her tongue around her lips in anticipation.

"Please tell me that 'hot dogs' is another case of botched translation," Tinka replied with a wary look. It turned out that Drazens, like practically all humanoid cultures, had been accompanied by dogs since their early development. That and the fact that certain dogs across the galaxy were capable of interbreeding had led scientists to propose two hypotheses. Either dogs were part of a spacefaring race that had regressed after colonizing compatible worlds, or canines had been seeded as part of some grand plan to which humanoids weren't privy.

"Yeah, hotdogs are really just over-processed mystery meat. There are human cultures that traditionally eat dog, but the Stryx have banned it on their stations, since they consider most dogs to be sentient and it's not practical to test them all."

"All the same, I think I'll stick with the snake," Tinka declared a little louder than she intended. A number of the boys around them shifted to a different line, so they arrived at the grill a little quicker than they might have otherwise.

"Everything go well?" Laurel asked happily. Although she was often uncomfortable with crowds in other social situations, as long as she was cooking she was in her element.

"It was a lot of fun," Chastity told her. "We basically stayed near Paul's raider and did whatever he said, just like in practice. I could live without the fighting altogether, but I need to make hours to keep my Trader profile active. This is Tinka, by the way."

"THE Tinka?" Laurel asked in a sotto voice.

"Hey, I was just protecting my charge," the Drazen girl replied unapologetically. Her attempt to claim asylum for the EarthCent ambassador's daughter had brought her a degree of instant fame among those with connections to the diplomatic community.

InstaSitter was receiving so many requests for Tinka's services that Blythe had created a new supervisory slot for the girl. The job was basically public relations, showing up at the homes of new clients with the actual babysitter for the night to "supervise" the meeting with the parents. This allowed InstaSitter to spread Tinka's time as thinly as possible, and the girl had proven a natural at easing the fears of new customers, especially since the Drazens were a known quantity to the older species.

Laurel turned a pair of chicken breasts with her tongs and brushed on a little more barbeque sauce. "These will be done in just a minute. I usually don't fall behind, but a lot of these guys really load up their plates rather than getting back in line for seconds. So what was it like, being the only girls playing with all these boys around?"

"We were in our mock-up the whole time," Chastity explained. "We got here early this morning for some extra coaching from Paul, so this is really the first time we're seeing any of them in the flesh. Most of them are Paul's age or older."

"And they smell funny," the Drazen girl added, causing the young men in line behind them to surreptitiously sniff at their clothing or exhale into a cupped hand and bring it rapidly to their noses.

"They do," fifteen-year old Chastity confirmed, and the girls crinkled their noses at each other and laughed.

"Just wait a few years and you'll get used to it," Laurel said, placing a chicken breast on a plate for each of them. "Make sure you try my three-bean salad, it's on the table between the corn and the potato salad. And I see Paul waiting by the beer keg with Dring, the cute dinosaur guy who's living on the other side of the scrap pile. You should go sit with them."

Chastity led Tinka around the back of the serving line to attack the salad table from the opposite side, but also to get away from the crush of young men who towered over the petite girl by more than a head, such that she couldn't see much other than backs and chests. From there they continued through the staff area until they reached the beer line, where Joe was pumping out his latest homebrew for hordes of willing guinea pigs.

"Hey, Uncle Joe," Chastity addressed the burgeoning brewmaster. "Paul say anything bad about us?"

"I can't imagine what he would have to complain about," Joe replied, pulling a pint of homebrew. The overflow dripped into a pan on the floor, which Beowulf licked clean as soon as there was enough to make the effort worthwhile. Joe handed the plastic cup to the next young man in line, did a quick check to make sure Kelly wasn't watching, and then pulled a short pint for each of the girls. As the cups filled, he introduced them to Dring, who was apparently enjoying his first human picnic, though like Chastity, he couldn't see over the men due to his diminutive stature.

"Ah, the younger sister of Paul's mate," Dring remarked. His fluency in English was impressive, but his grasp of social mores still suffered gaps. "A very interesting girl, your sister. I was taken by her business acumen and her instinctive grasp of complex systems. So are the two of you here to select mates of your own?"

Chastity, who was never flustered, simply ignored the question, but the Drazen girl turned a pale shade of green and mumbled something about interspecies relations that didn't translate coherently. Paul came to the rescue by herding the group off towards a table with enough open spots for them all to sit together.

Everybody they moved past congratulated Paul and slapped his back. One group of players, who had strategically chosen an early trip through the beer line over food and had already been back for refills, broke into a playful rendition of, "For he's a jolly good fellow."

"The six hours you logged today will keep your Trader profiles active for a month, unless you've started living in a mock-up," Paul addressed both girls. "Are you going to start flying regular missions with us, or just come in as replacements when you're running short?"

"We haven't really talked about it yet," Chastity answered. "It was fun, but if it's six hours every week, that's probably more than either of us can afford. I'd end up spending all of my game time fighting and not get any trading done!"

Tinka, who in addition to working for InstaSitter was attending the Drazen equivalent of finishing school, nodded her agreement.

"Around a quarter of these guys are in the same boat," Paul told them. "That's why we use the replacements system, so we can accommodate the players who can only go on missions once in a while. It will be even more flexible when we integrate the squadron with the new Earth fleet."

"A larger system?" Dring looked up from his careful dissection of the three-bean salad, which along with some raw carrot and celery sticks, was all that he had found of interest in the food line. "Is there a purpose to joining a larger body, or are you just imitating the natural evolution of militarized cultures?"

"It's just sort of happening," Paul admitted. "If you had asked six months ago, the squadron flying out of this barn today might have been the biggest Raider fleet in the galaxy. But the game keeps expanding, and as it does, the squadrons end up joining fleets and armadas. I imagine by the end of the year we'll be fighting fleet actions in the gameverse that are bigger than anything that's ever happened in the real universe. That is, if the Stryxnet can keep up with the data traffic."

"I wouldn't worry about the Stryx end of things," Dring replied with a dismissive snort. Either that or he was having trouble swallowing the celery stick that he had barely chewed. "It's more likely your individual ship controllers will go into saturation. What kind of numbers are we talking about?"

"Millions," Paul said, with a bit of awe in his tone. "Maybe tens of millions. It seems like every gamer in the galaxy is playing this game, so even if only a few percent of them have the time and the upgrades to join a squadron, the fleets will still be enormous."

"Extraordinary," Dring said. "I really must stay around and see how this system evolves. I'm sure there must be something more to it than simple entertainment."

"Blythe says it's modeling," Chastity mentioned in an off-hand manner. "She said if we were still in the flower business and we wanted to expand it beyond the station, Raider/Trader would have been an excellent planning tool. It doesn't apply to InstaSitter, though. Babysitting is strictly local."

"Our guys all say that it's almost as good as the war gaming in the Drazen fleet academy." Tinka looked like she was about to say something more, but she took another sip of Joe's homebrew instead. "This really tastes pretty good and I like the fizz. I don't think my dad would go for it, though. Not toxic enough."

Eight

The biggest draw at the Earth Exposition was the EarthCent booth, where Kelly was wearing out her hand signing repurposed vaccination certificates that authorized the alien bearer to engage in commercial transactions on Earth. The certificates served no legal purpose since EarthCent didn't restrict aliens from engaging in Earth commerce to start with, but none of the local species were willing to make the long trip without a bureaucratic ace in the pocket. It seemed that the older the species, the more careful they were about preparing paperwork when visiting backwards planets.

"I should have made you a rubber stamp," Donna told Kelly sympathetically, as she broke open another sheaf of certificates. "All the same, did you ever think we would have too many species knocking on our door?"

Kelly groaned and arched her back, trying to loosen up her overused shoulder muscles. It was amazing how just signing your name over and over again could put such a strain on the upper body. She had started shifting back and forth between left-handed and right-handed after the first hour, though not even her mother could have recognized the scrawl that resulted when she used her off hand. Thankfully, Donna was there to take notes about the diplomats who were ready to upgrade their relations with

Earth, and Libby was recording the whole event for EarthCent as well.

The evening started well for Kelly, with a long streak of positive identifications of species, thanks to her two weeks of cramming with holo slides. But then a wave of unknowns had hit, some of them wearing elaborate protective suits, because the air was just too different from their native environment to breathe or gill with simple filters. The last half an hour had mainly consisted of ambulatory nightmares that Kelly had never dreamed could exist, and there seemed to be an endless supply. She comforted herself with the thought that none of the extreme examples showed an interest in inviting her to dinner.

Despite her twenty years of service as an EarthCent diplomat, it was the first time she had really experienced the centrality of the Stryx stations to galactic diplomacy. It simply didn't make sense for any of the species to try to maintain a diplomatic presence on every populated world, much less those with atmospheres or oceans that were poison for them. But every species that had any interest in trade relations with the bulk of galactic civilizations, somewhere above sixty percent by Gryph's estimate, maintained an embassy on the major Stryx stations near the hubs of the tunnel network. Diplomats from every social species were never more than a lift tube ride away from face-to-face meetings.

"Great Expo," Joe said, materializing behind Kelly and starting to massage her shoulders with his large, calloused hands. Kelly groaned out loud and briefly considered passing out from pleasure. But the line of jostling aliens didn't magically disappear, though at least it no longer extended right out the door of the Nebulae room and into the Empire Convention Center lobby. There would be plenty of time to pass out in her LoveU massaging recliner when the night was over.

"Are the aliens, I mean, are our guests actually going around to the other booths, or are they just grabbing their certificates and leaving?" she asked Joe. "I can't see a thing sitting here."

"I'd say it's a big hit," Joe assured her. "I wish I'd brought some beer and tried to drum up orders, but Laurel and her friends are doing a bang-up business with their 'Tastes of Our Home World' smorgasbord. I've seen some pretty spectacular digestive failures and allergic reactions taking place in the dining area, but I guess the smart travelers would rather get it out of the way here, with their own medical staff available."

"Ugh," Kelly grunted, making a note to herself not to use the bathroom until she got home. "How about the girls from the Shuk? Are they getting a crowd?"

"Can't you hear them from over here?" Joe asked, and cocked his head to listen. "I guess not, this is a noisy bunch. They've been taking orders nonstop. Those two with the black hair who look like clones? They could have been drill sergeants with those lungs. You don't want to know what I saw a humanoid with a purple octopus head doing with a nutcracker, though."

"Too much information," Kelly told him, as she signed another certificate for a humanoid with a green octopus for a head, reminding her of a Hydra illustration from a children's book.

"How are my girls doing?" Donna asked.

"Second biggest crowd in the place," Joe replied with a grin. "They brought Tinka along to help, and believe it or not, the poor girl is probably signing as many autographs

73

as Kelly. Come to think of it, I think some of them were asking her to add her name to the same certificate."

Kelly bent low over the table while signing the next batch of documents so that her husband and best friend wouldn't see her expression. It's not like human parents all over the galaxy don't pretend to nibble on their children's toes or ears, she fumed to herself. And now Blythe had turned it into a marketing coup for InstaSitter. Next thing I'll be hearing about it from Earth!

There was a ding in her ear, and the words, "Collect call from Mother," appeared floating before her eyes.

"Accept charges," Kelly subvoced, switching hands again as she blindly signed another certificate. The current batch of supplicants were encased in armored environmental suits and approached the table one by one with an articulated metal arm extended, not even attempting a word of small talk. Whatever her mother had to say, it would beat listening to Joe and Donna carrying on about the entrepreneurial girls.

"How's my ambassadorial daughter?"

"I'm fine, Mom. I can't talk long, though. I'm working."

"Friday evening? I understand if you're stretched for money, dear, but taking on a part-time job to make ends meet at your age isn't very sensible," her mother said seriously. "I thought you said that Joe was doing well these days."

"He is, Mother. I'm not at a part-time job. I'm running an Earth Exposition, meeting hundreds of important aliens. In fact, I really can't talk long."

"That's all right, just listen. Your father and I have decided we could use a little vacation, so he's going fishing out West with your brother's father-in-law at the end of next month, and I'm coming to see you. Isn't that great?"

Kelly's hair would have stood up on end if she wasn't so tired. Her shoulders suddenly tensed under Joe's hands, causing him to jerk to attention and study the group of aliens waving their arms in his wife's face. But the ambassador was continuing the great paper giveaway on autopilot, so he relaxed back into rubbing her shoulders while listening to Donna talk about the kids. Apparently, the reason Paul had offered to babysit Dorothy for the evening was to get out of helping at the InstaSitter booth, and Blythe wasn't happy about it.

"Mom, you know I really want to see you. But it's a multi-day trip, and some of it is in zero gravity. You've never even been off the planet before. Are you sure you're up to it?"

"I've already booked a cruise, Kelly. The new orbital elevators make it easy to get off the planet without being crushed by acceleration, and they say that it's statistically safer than walking. I'll only be on Union Station for a week, but we're stopping at all of the exotic ports on the tunnel network along the way. I got a great discount through our seniors group."

"Oh," Kelly let slip, then gave herself a mental slap and tried to sound bright. "Well, send me your itinerary, and I can't wait to see you."

"That's what I wanted to hear. And Kelly, do me a favor and don't devour my tasty little granddaughter before I get to see her."

"What?" Kelly said out loud, rising to her feet and causing the remaining few aliens in line to surge forward as a group for fear that they were going to miss out. "Mom! How did you mean that?" But her mother had already cut the connection, a first in Kelly's memory.

"What's wrong, Kel?" Joe asked, as Kelly slumped back into her chair and the final group of supplicants nervously reformed a line. "Was I squeezing too hard? Did I hit a nerve?"

"Just a collect call from my mother," Kelly replied, sounding defeated. "She's coming to visit at the end of next month."

"That's great," Donna and Joe both said in chorus.

"I've always wanted to meet her," Joe added, unsure why Kelly suddenly looked so depressed. "I thought you got along well with her."

"With a galaxy between us, sure. But she has a way of getting under my skin when we're in the same room. She finds fault with everything I do, and..." Kelly paused when she realized there was nobody behind the large ant-like creature extending a limb. She signed the last repurposed vaccination certificate with a flourish and stuck it on the pointy appendage. The creature bowed its head and scurried out the door.

"And she said something about me not eating Dorothy before she gets here," Kelly groused.

"Ouch, all the way back to Earth," Joe marveled. "Well, they say it's better to be infamous than anonymous."

Donna hid a smile behind her hand and began straightening out the mess of leftover certificates for future use. "I'll just keep a few of these out, Kelly, for any late arrivals, but you may as well stretch your legs and take a look around. It really was a huge success, you know. I'll bet you have a formal dinner reception invitation from every nitrogen/oxygen breathing species on the station."

"They probably just want to see if I eat anything other than children," Kelly replied sourly. But her mood was already brightening, and she accepted Joe's invitation to take a stroll around the exposition hall.

Once she was out from behind the table, Kelly felt a surge of pride at what they had accomplished. Representatives from more species than she could ever recall seeing in the same room at the same time milled around the spacious hall, stopping at the booths around the edges, or congregating in the central food court area where they sampled Earth staples and delicacies alike. The scene was only made more colorful by a band of normally staid Tharks doing an intoxicated line dance as they licked at sample bars of imported handmade soap from Anne's Boutique.

As Joe had reported, there was a big crowd at the InstaSitter booth, where the demand was so great that Blythe had called in Thomas to help. Kelly couldn't prevent herself from imagining one side of the dialogue between the naïve artificial person and a prospective client:

"Yes, I've sat for the ambassador. No, she's really very nice and I've never seen her eat anyone. Yes, you can have my autograph on the certificate also if you think it will help with something."

Some angry shouts and jostling erupted from the packed crowd in front of the Fight On booth, where Donna's husband was attempting to calm the excited gamers. When Stanley spotted Joe over the heads of the crowd, he immediately beckoned for him to come over, and said something to the antagonists that put them on their best behavior. While Kelly was reluctant to let go of Joe, she didn't have the energy left to remain on her feet through a heated discussion about some obscure gaming protocol. So she gave him a push in the right direction, and headed for the Shuk booths to check in with the Hadad family.

"This is Joe McAllister," Stanley introduced Joe to the crowd of fractious aliens. "He owns the Raider/Trader barn that supports the squadron you're asking about. His son Paul is the Nova champion who commands the squadron, so maybe he can help with your questions."

"Is it true that the new Earth fleet intends to ally with the Vergallian/Drazen axis to attack the Dollnicks?" demanded a tall Dolly, his four hands clenched in fists.

"Attack the Dollnicks? In the gameverse?" Joe asked incredulously. "Look, I never heard of Earth participating in any grand interspecies alliances in the gameverse before you brought it up. Besides, the way I understand it, everybody has to get their fighting hours in to maintain their game profile, so what difference does it make?"

"What did he just say? Does he expect us to believe that?" The bunched up mass of gamers surged forward with what passed for ugly expressions on their faces, and Stanley got ready to pull his baseball bat out of the Velcro loops securing it to the bottom of the booth table. Fortunately, Patches arrived back from the "Tastes of Our Home World" booth, and after a lightning assessment of the situation, launched into a flood of indecipherable barn banter.

"Squadron commander sliced a loaf with Big Bird, and they're looking glass for the pow-wow in the shallow deeps. If the rocks scatter and the wrappers pay bills, we'll all be in the basket come the Big One."

Satisfied with his own explanation, Patches transferred his attention to the giant sandwich Laurel had made for him, and showed no inclination to explain further. Oddly enough, the various translation implants employed by the species present must have come up with something that satisfied the opposing parties, because the tension drained from the mob. Stanley removed his hand from the bat handle.

"Any idea what the kid just said?" Joe asked his friend in an undertone.

"I was going to ask you," Stanley replied. "It's your barn, after all. These gameverse alliance rumors are starting to become a real issue. I thought humans did so well at games because we take them so seriously, but the Raider/Trader wars are taking on a life of their own."

"Just don't let it spill over into the Expo," Joe cautioned him, as a pair of Frunge sidled up to the table on their root-like feet, hoping to get an answer about the rules for an old human board game that one of them held. "This is a big night for Kelly and I don't want it spoiled by a riot. She's been kind of sensitive since the Tinka incident."

Joe left the Fight On booth and headed over to the section taken up by Shuk vendors, who made up a good third of the Earth businesses with booths. The exposition format was ideal for the merchants who grew up in open-air style markets, competing mainly on presentation and salesmanship. Kelly was already at the Kitchen Kitsch booth, engaged in a deep conversation with Peter and Shaina, while Brinda kept the traffic coming with her piercing alto.

"Nutcrackers, nutcrackers, nutcrackers. Shirts and skirts, shoes and ties. Kitchen Kitsch has the latest Earth fashions, so you won't offend human eyes. Nutcrackers, nutcrackers, nutcrackers."

"Joe. Good. Listen to what Peter has been telling me. Do you mind repeating it, Peter?" Kelly had the bright-eyed look that Joe had come to associate with working on a mystery. Solving puzzles made Kelly happy, and a happy

Kelly made Joe happy, so the evening was definitely looking up.

"Well, Shaina could tell it better I guess. I've been running back and forth to the warehouse for more supplies, and I really should squeeze in one more trip," the Hadad patriarch said, with a nervous look at the rapidly diminishing stock behind the booth. Shaina wasn't one to wait for a second invitation, and she launched into the story as her father headed for the exit, a string of mulebots floating in his wake.

"I grew up doing business with all of the species who can stand the atmosphere on the Shuk deck, and I'm usually decent at reading between the lines in negotiations," the young woman began modestly. "So it was a real surprise to me when some Dollys I know brought around one of their merchant princes, who they said just happened to be on the station. The Dollys are hardly the oldest or the most powerful species in the sector, at best they're middle of the pack, but when it comes to concentration of wealth, the old four-arms are at the top of the pyramid. Their extended families pay a sort of tithe, it's a cross between insurance and a protection racket, but the point is, there's a small group at the top who have mountains of Stryx creds."

"They're already super rich?" Kelly interrupted Shaina's lecture. "So why should they care about chasing after Earth's newfound wealth?"

Shaina gave Kelly a look of pity, and Joe just sighed and shrugged. Thanks to a life in government service, Kelly was a bit thick about business.

"Nobody stays rich by running away from opportunities," Shaina explained patiently. "When this prince started talking, I thought he was trying to sound us out for investment opportunities in the Earth export business. You know, to get an idea of what we're selling, maybe extend a fake offer of partnership to worm information about profit margins out of us, the usual thing. But instead he comes on like a salesman, telling me about a limited partnership for mining platinum on some moon that I could buy into for just a couple billion creds. He wanted introductions to our backers on Earth, if you can believe that."

"A couple billion Stryx creds?" Kelly repeated. "That's like the EarthCent operating budget, well, forever. Where did he expect you to come up with that money?"

Shaina shrugged her narrow shoulders and continued. "So I watched him work the room for a while, which was easy, since he must be the tallest alien on the station. Then I did a quick walk-about and talked to the vendors at the booths he visited, and they all reported the same experience. This merchant prince is approaching Shuk vendors and mom-n-pop importers like we're all made of money or we have a rich uncle back on Earth. That's when I realized that customers from some of the other species who were buying bits of this or that were hinting at the same thing. They're just subtler. I hadn't put two and two together before because it's so ridiculous."

"Well, I know from the Stryx that money has been pouring into Earth the last few months, and apparently everybody else knows as well. You just explained to me that the Dollnicks operate on a tithe system with the deep pockets at the top, so maybe he figured it must be the same with humans. It makes sense that a Dolly prince would want to do business with an Earth business magnate."

"I guess," Shaina replied, surprised that she hadn't made the connection herself. "But what about that other thing my Dad told you about, the new wholesale consortium? We still specialize in Earth imports, but we've added some off-world items, like the nose filters from the Chintoo orbital complex that just work better than the old ones. The consortium trader took Angora wool in barter, which I can't imagine the robots running Chintoo need for anything."

"Better nose filters?" Kelly asked hopefully.

Shaina smiled and gave Kelly a friendly elbow bump. "My sister Brinda has a couple pairs in her pocket for you. I was going to send her over when things slowed down but you got here first. Great Expo, by the way. Hey, Joe."

"Hey, Shaina," Joe responded and threw in an obligatory gentle elbow. "If you're finished with the Ambassador, I thought I'd treat her to a meal."

"Good idea, just steer clear of the restrooms," Shaina advised them seriously. "And Kelly, make sure you give a good tip to the maintenance staff. They're going to earn it tonight."

Nine

Kelly sat cross-legged next to Dorothy and hoped that her forty-year-old knees would cooperate and not make gunshot noises when it was her turn to get up and talk. Still, it was fun sitting in the grass, surrounded by four and five-year-old children, and an equal number of little Stryx. The kindergarten was a new addition to the Stryx-run school which had previously started with six-year-olds, so Dorothy's class was a sort of an experiment. One or two parents sat next to each child for Parents Day, and the little Stryx were scattered among the humans, often near a particular friend. Metoo stood on Dorothy's other side, and Kelly noticed that her daughter patted the little robot from time to time, as if to console him for not bringing a parent.

Joe had warned Kelly that parental show-and-tells at Stryx school could be a nerve-wracking experience, but she was sure now that he must have been pulling her leg. He had even advised her to prepare an activity or to bring the dog to give the children rides, as if she couldn't keep a few children entertained by talking about her job. Why, the father of one child, an astrophysicist by profession, had spent his entire five-minute slot blowing up balloons, then exclaiming, "Go rocket! Go!" and then releasing them to zoom around the room. All of the children had taken up the chant, even the little Stryx, and they seemed to enjoy watching the man turn red blowing up the balloons as much as following the erratic flights. This would be a piece of cake.

Breathless, but otherwise looking pleased with himself, the rocket man handed the presentation baton to a woman sitting with a cardboard box and a folded tray table. She quickly rose and moved to the front of the assembly. With practiced motions, the woman unfolded the tray table and poured out the contents of the box, consisting of a large number of plastic containers with different color caps. She assumed an unnaturally serious expression as she opened each container, casting a speculative look at a different child as she removed each cap, as if she were measuring the children to see if they would fit inside. The woman was a good actress and the anticipation in the room grew.

"Ready!" she finally announced. "I'm Yafu's mother and I work as a Xenobiologist. What that means is...," the woman paused dramatically and arched her eyebrows, "I make monsters!"

All of the children squealed and grabbed at the nearest adult or a robot friend, and Kelly was awarded one of Dorothy's hands, even as the other grabbed one of Metoo's pincers.

"So who wants to be a monster?" the Xenobiologist asked, and everybody present, including a few overly enthusiastic parents, shouted, "Me! Me!"

"No big monsters today, I'd need something to stand on," Yafu's mother scolded the adults. "How about five volunteers to start, and anybody else who wants to be a monster can see me after our picnic lunch. Who wants to go first?"

Being the first to become a monster must have struck the children as a little scary, because all of the hands went down. The monster maker pointed dramatically at a little boy of Chinese ancestry, who gamely rose and approached to face his mother, his back to the class. She worked quickly, dipping her small fingers directly into the face paint pots, and she moved so smoothly and with such concentration, it almost looked like she was playing a small piano. In less than a minute, she stepped back and held up her hands, each finger a different color, and whispered to Yafu to turn around.

The class gasped on seeing how his face had been transformed into that of a giant bird. She had even used shadowing to make his tiny nose look like a prominent beak, and his eyes appeared to be twice their normal size. The parents broke out in applause and started pushing their children towards the front of the class. The first volunteer to reach the artist was a little blonde girl with such a beautiful, bright complexion that the woman hesitated to cover it up. Then she assumed a mad scientist expression, leered crazily at the class, and set to work.

A minute later the little girl turned around and a mother shrieked and then began laughing hysterically. Half of the girl's face was untouched, and the other half looked like a wolf, complete with fangs and half of a lolling tongue reaching down her chin. The creamy white skin on the wolf side was replaced with the illusion of fine grey fur, and one of her baby blue eyes even seemed to have acquired a yellow tint. The artist hadn't quite managed to pull off the effect of a protruding snout on just one side of the face, but it was a miraculous transformation all the same, and everybody cheered again.

In rapid succession the next three children were transformed into mythical creatures, and Kelly began to pray that she wouldn't be the next to receive the presentation baton. Fortunately, the woman handed the baton, which looked like a child's magic wand complete with a paper star on one end, to the small, unassuming man who sat on Kelly's right. The father, who looked like he might have been a clerk in a small office, rose nervously to his feet, gave his daughter's hand a squeeze, and introduced himself.

"Hi! I'm Sarah's dad, and I'm an agronomist. That's just a big word to say I grow food." Then, without moving from his place, he began to sing:

Old MacDonald had a farm, E-I-E-I-O
And on that farm he had a snake, E-I-E-I-O
With a hiss hiss here, and a hiss hiss there
Here a hiss, there a hiss, everywhere a hiss hiss
Old MacDonald had a farm, E-I-E-I-O

By the time he got to the end of the second line, all of the children and little Stryx were singing along. At the end of the verse, he pointed at a random child who instinctively knew what to do and shouted "Chicken." The man launched into the next verse with a cluck cluck, and before Kelly knew it, she was singing along with the rest of them.

Old MacDonald went well over the five minutes allotted before the man pointed at a little Stryx, who suggested a spider. All of the children laughed, and Kelly overheard the little boy sitting next to the Stryx explain to his robotic friend, "The spider lives in a different song, the one with the rain and the waterspout."

The agronomist yielded the presentation baton to Kelly, and sat down looking flushed and happy. Kelly rose gracefully to her feet, though her knees made sounds like a boxer cracking his knuckles, and moved to the front of the group.

"Hi everybody. I'm Dorothy's mother Kelly, and I'm the EarthCent ambassador on Union Station. Does everybody know what an ambassador does?"

Blank looks from all of the children were her only answer, so she turned to Dorothy and said, "Dorothy? Do you want to tell the children what an ambassador does?"

Dorothy stood up proudly and said, "A 'bassador tells me when to go to bed and not to eat tasty things." Then she sat back down and received an admiring look from Metoo. Kelly thought about asking her to try again, but decided it would be less confusing if she talked directly to the children.

"An ambassador is somebody who talks with different people and different species to promote understanding," Kelly explained, but the sea of blank little faces remained unimpressed. Some of the parents began to show signs of conducting subvoced conversations over implants or reading from their heads-up displays. Twenty seconds and she was already losing her audience. Kelly began to panic.

"When I was taking diplomacy instruction, no wait, sorry, I'll start over." Kelly struggled to regain her composure and to ignore the parents. That's the problem, she thought. I'm trying to talk to everybody when I should just be talking to the children. She concentrated on her daughter and tried again. "We used to play a game in ambassador school where we made friends. Does anybody want to play?"

All of the little hands went up, and all of the little Stryx pincers as well. Her confidence rushing back, Kelly tried to recall if she had learned anything in the EarthCent course that she could explain to a four or five-year-old. One of the little boys was holding a stuffed animal in the hand that wasn't waving wildly over his head, so she pointed and invited him up. For the other half of the equation, she chose a girl from the front who was probably the biggest child in the room.

"What's your name?" she asked the little boy, who grew suddenly shy and even tried to hide his face behind her leg.

"Xavier," the boy's mother answered for him from the crowd.

"And your name is?" she asked the girl.

"Bekka!" the girl asserted stoutly.

"Are you friends Xavier and Bekka?" Kelly asked, like a magician establishing that she hid nothing up her sleeves before performing a trick. Bekka shrugged, while Xavier shook his head energetically to indicate the negative.

"Good," Kelly continued. "We're going to learn how to make friends. Now Xavier, I want you to give Bekka your Teddy Bear. Bekka, I want you to take it from him."

Xavier looked at Kelly horror-stuck and tried to back away from the girl, but Kelly placed a restraining hand on his shoulder.

"It's just an ambassador game," she cajoled him. "Don't you want to play?"

Xavier stared at her wide-eyed and looked like he was about to burst into tears. Just as Kelly was about to admit failure and ask for another volunteer, Bekka leaned forward and seized one of the Teddy Bear's legs, trying to jerk it away from the boy. The leg came off with a rip, and stuffing spilled out on the grass. Xavier began to howl.

"No! No, Bekka. Wait! We can still make friends," Kelly pleaded, looking back and forth between the two children. "Give him back the leg and tell him you're sorry."

"But you told me to take it!" Bekka wailed, and threw the lifeless leg at Kelly's feet. Oddly enough, as Bekka rapidly worked herself up into a full-blown tantrum, Xavier began to calm down and stare at her curiously. At this point, the parents of the respective children stalked up to the front to retrieve their offspring. Bekka's father picked her up to comfort her, and strode away from the group with a disgusted look at Kelly.

"Oh, I'm sorry. That didn't go very well, did it, children." Kelly hadn't meant it as a question, but the children chorused, "No!"

"Well, maybe we can try another ambassador game with just one player so nobody can get hurt. Shall we?" Kelly asked hopefully. This time she expected the children to answer "Yes," but the room was silent.

"Can I have a volunteer?" she asked, trying not to sound too needy. One little girl in a white dress began to raise her hand, but her mother intercepted it on the way up and pulled it back down. Kelly was about to give up and beckon to Dorothy, who was sitting on her hands and looking nervous, when Metoo raised a tentative pincer.

"Metoo! Great, come up here. Everybody give Metoo a hand." A few of the adults clapped once or twice, but the children sat and looked puzzled, obviously not understanding what Kelly was talking about. She gave herself another mental kick—watch the vocabulary!

Metoo bravely floated up to Kelly, though she thought he might be wobbling a little. "Hi, Metoo," she greeted him, trying her best to sound enthusiastic. "We're going to play a little game that teaches you about problems between people. All you have to do is make believe what I tell you is true. Do you understand? It's just make believe."

"Yes," Metoo rasped nervously, sounding more artificial than usual.

"Good. Now I want you to pretend that I won't let you be friends with Dorothy anymore. How do you..." Kelly was interrupted by the clatter of Metoo collapsing onto the grass in a metallic pile. Dorothy screamed and charged forward to dive on top of the fallen Stryx, and some of the children began to sob.

"It's just make believe," Kelly shouted over the noise, trying to get Metoo's attention, but the little Stryx wasn't responsive and just lay there in a heap. "Libby! Help!" she subvoced urgently. "I think Metoo turned himself off or something."

"He put himself to sleep," Libby reported back almost instantly. "Young Stryx will do that if they learn something horrible. It's why we don't let them around humans for their first few years."

"Tell me what I can do!" Kelly urged her, almost in tears herself.

"Take him home with you, and I'll send Jeeves to meet you and wake him up. Make sure that Dorothy is there so he doesn't just go to sleep again," Libby instructed her. Kelly grimaced as she realized that Libby had watched the whole performance. "I'll reactivate his suspension field so you can carry him easily, just make sure you don't let go somewhere that he can float out of reach."

"Dorothy, Dorothy," Kelly tried to pry her daughter off the prone robot. "Metoo is just sleeping. Mommy talked to Libby and we're taking him home to wake him up."

Dorothy wouldn't let go, and Kelly wanted to get Metoo out of the room before she inflicted a permanent trauma on the whole class, so she scooped them up in one load, half of it squirming, half of it limp. Metoo weighed nothing, in fact his suspensor field may have been supporting some of Dorothy's weight. Kelly headed for the door mumbling apologies.

Behind her, a quick-thinking mother rose to her feet and asked, "Who wants to play with a puppy?" The sobbing stopped immediately, and even the little Stryx perked up again in anticipation. The woman held her large purse near the floor, undid the clasp, and out popped a cute little spaniel, its bright red tongue licking in every direction. As the door slid shut behind her, Kelly admitted to herself that she should have taken Joe's advice to bring Beowulf and let the giant dog give the children pony back rides.

Ten

A week after what had become known around the human section of the station as "The Kindergarten Incident," Metoo was still proudly wearing a whole box worth of animal-themed band-aids that Dorothy had carefully applied wherever she found an open spot on his indestructible robot casing. In order to be forgiven, Kelly had solemnly functioned as nurse to her daughter's role as surgeon, removing the band-aids from their pesky sleeves and peeling off the waxed portions that protected the sticky surfaces.

Joe was watching Dorothy and Metoo playing with blocks in the corner of the living room when Jeeves pinged to ask if he was available for a discussion. Since Joe was babysitting while Kelly attended a meeting of Earth merchants, he was happy to oblige. Jeeves arrived in less than a minute, which meant he must have been in the corridor when he called.

"I see Metoo is healing nicely," Jeeves told Dorothy. "What a good doctor you are." Dorothy responded with a happy smile and hugged Metoo, who basked in the attention. "And no more going to sleep when you're upset," Jeeves admonished the little Stryx sternly. "You're getting too big for that kind of behavior."

"I'm getting bigger even faster," Joe commented from the couch, where he sat with a mug of his latest homebrew and a bag of mini-pretzels. Beowulf lay supine on the couch next to him, his massive body taking up the rest of the cushion space and his heavy head resting on the man's lap. The dog only showed signs of life if a pretzel was placed on his tongue, in which case he made it disappear as quickly as a frog ingests a fly, and then fanned the air once or twice with his tail.

Jeeves floated over and took his time giving the man and the dog a thorough examination. "As a field agent for Eemas on loan to InstaSitter, I can say with a certainty that neither of you would qualify to work for us. One is swilling beer on duty and the other can barely keep his eyes open. I'd be nervous about Metoo remaining here if I didn't know that Dorothy would keep an eye on him."

"Well, if it isn't the InstaTraitor," Joe replied, having become immune to the robot's constant put-downs and giving as well as he received. "What's this I hear about you hanging around a Frunge barn trying to sell our Raider/Trader secrets?"

"You heard wrong, though I suppose it's a miracle you can hear anything at your advanced age," Jeeves retorted. Beowulf opened his eyes and growled, leading Jeeves to add, "I was talking about Joe." Mollified, the dog went back to his daydreams.

"So what were you doing with the Shrubs? Looking to get a good deal on counterfeit robot parts?" Joe drained the rest of his beer, feeling rather pleased with his own gibe. Strangely enough, Jeeves omitted a comeback and launched into a serious explanation.

"There's something funny about this new game. Gryph has been talking with the Stryx who run stations, and they all agree that it's more than entertainment. Gryph and Libby have put me in charge of investigating the human-related angle, since I'm supposed to understand your illogical culture better than the mature Stryx."

"Everybody's heard rumors," Joe replied with a shrug and a longing look at his empty glass. But Kelly wouldn't let him keep a keg in the living room, and he didn't feel like going downstairs to his micro-brewery room. Or to be truthful, he didn't have the energy to pry Beowulf's head up off his lap when he would only have to fight with the dog a minute later to win back his end of the sofa.

"Thank you, Joe. That was very useful," the Stryx replied sarcastically. "The reason I'm talking to you rather than Paul is that we're seeing some interesting patterns developing in mercenary deployments."

Joe sat up a little straighter when Jeeves mentioned the mercenaries. There was nothing glamorous about the fighting business, but for a poor twenty-year-old human with no family, it had seemed like a better option than signing a labor contract for an agricultural or mining colony. Joe had worked his way up from the bottom as a soldier of fortune, contracting to aliens for fighting in space and on planets across the galaxy. He had seventeen years of service, basically long stretches of waiting or traveling on troopships, punctuated by short periods of lethal violence. Then he had won Mac's Bones in a card game and retired to the junkyard business, in part to give his war-orphan foster son a place to call home.

"What kind of patterns?" Joe asked, now that Jeeves had his attention.

"We've seen mercenary units which have always contracted independently, now concentrating together near transportation hubs which are anchored by a Stryx station. They report being offered longer term retainers with guaranteed leave time and a maximum number of combat hours per cycle. For the time being, the consortium that's coordinating this activity appears to be acting as a middleman for the traditional mercenary customers. Since the pay and hire rates are unchanged, the consortium is probably operating at a loss."

"You're crazy if you suspect they're planning some move against the stations," Joe said dismissively. "It doesn't matter who is paying. There isn't a human soldier in the galaxy dumb enough to go against the Stryx, even if you weren't our patrons. I'll bet with the right accessories you could take us all on single-handedly."

"I might need both hands," Jeeves replied modestly. "But the reason these forces are concentrating near the Stryx stations is simply to lower transportation costs and ensure rapid deployment options. We don't see any sign of a change in the pattern of ongoing conflicts, or even in the diplomatic stand-offs that are often preludes to shooting wars. It's strictly a question of the business model changing, and it's not just human mercenaries who are signing on."

"I haven't really kept up with my old crowd," Joe confessed. "Some of the men from the last unit I commanded will stop in for a beer when they pass through Union, but it wasn't a life that encouraged long-term friendships. The only way I could get caught up would be to visit one of those staging worlds, and from what you've said, I'm not sure there's anything to be learned."

"I'd like you to come with me to visit the local mustering point which has been forming around Zach's World in recent months. We can take the Nova, and with some help from Gryph, it's only a few hours away. While most mercenaries are willing enough to talk with Stryx, it would add credibility if you came along. We might even ask Kelly to give you an official position."

"Let me think about it for a minute," Joe answered, looking over at his daughter playing with Metoo. Kelly would probably be nervous about him going, but being accompanied by Jeeves was like traveling with an invasion fleet, or two invasion fleets if the Stryx was willing to use both hands. Besides, Joe felt he was getting a little too fat and happy sitting around the station, attending diplomatic dinners with Kelly and counting the creds flowing in from the barn. It didn't even take a full minute.

"I'll have to check with my wife, of course, but I'm willing," he told Jeeves.

"Good. I know you tend to sleep through flights whenever I'm along, so let's take the time now to get our plans straight. Have you been to Zach's World?"

"I always intended to go take a look, but with Paul and the business, and then Kelly and the girl, it just never happened," Joe admitted. Most of the human expats living on Union Station had made at least one trip to Zach's World, an icy ball with deep, slushy oceans and an oxygen-rich atmosphere that circled the star closest to the station. It offered a poor man's skiing vacation for those who didn't mind the too-gentle slopes, the weak red light from the distant parent star, and the cold, biting winds.

Nobody had ever tried engineering a heating cycle on Zach's World for three reasons. First, the breathable atmosphere depended on the biological processes of the plant life in the oceans, and those wouldn't have survived a higher temperature. Second, if the ice on the planet was melted, practically the entire surface would have ended up deep underwater. Third, the Stryx had declared the planet off limits for terraformers, rendering the first two reasons moot.

"There's never been enough traffic to the planet's surface to construct an elevator," Jeeves explained. "It's really not much different from living on a station, since the food is grown in greenhouses with artificial lighting. The staging base is on the high plains, where the dry air is easiest on the landing craft. Other than the proximity to the Stryx tunnel hub and the breathable atmosphere for humans, the main attraction is the gravity, which is just a few percent above Earth normal."

"So I'll wear warm socks," Joe replied impatiently, wondering why Jeeves was wasting so much time on the obvious.

"Aside from cold-weather training and equipment maintenance, there's not much to do on the high plains, other than snowboat sailing," Jeeves hinted. "I expect they do a lot of sitting about, telling old war stories, eating and drinking."

At the mention of drinking, Joe looked wistfully at his empty mug. At times he wished the dog had thumbs and could fetch a beer, though on second thought, if Beowulf had thumbs, their roles might be reversed entirely. Something clicked in Joe's mind.

"Are you suggesting that I bring a few kegs of homebrew along?" he asked Jeeves.

"In vino veritas," Jeeves responded, without explicitly answering in the affirmative.

"Is this another one of those self-imposed Stryx rules, like you aren't supposed to encourage alcohol exports from the station or something?" Joe asked the question out of frustration that Jeeves hadn't simply come out and told him to bring beer to the party.

"We try to avoid any actions that could be construed as helping humans at the expense of other species, especially in the economic realm," Jeeves replied vaguely. "For example, knowledge of trade routes and local demand is as valuable to merchants as the goods themselves. Who would use our tunnel network to transport commercial cargos if we were to share the specifics with their competitors?"

"Seems to me you take it a little too far at times."

"Hey, I'm new around here," Jeeves snapped, reminding Joe that the seemingly all-powerful robot was actually Paul's age. "I don't make the rules. Speaking of which, let me know if you get permission from your better nine-tenths."

Having successfully communicated the core of his strategy for the mission, that Joe bring along a load of beer to loosen up some lips, Jeeves took his leave from the children and floated out the exit. In doing so, he almost ran straight through Dring, who was visiting to return a book he had borrowed from Kelly's collection. Dring hopped to the side to avoid being run down, and followed the retreating figure of the Stryx with his eyes, his blunt teeth exposed in a half-regretful smile.

"Surprising creatures, your Stryx," he remarked to Joe conversationally, as if the robots were human pets and not the other way around. "It may be interesting to sit down and have a conversation with one someday."

"I'm sure Metoo would be happy to oblige," Joe responded jokingly. He pointed to the band-aid covered robot, whose delicately balanced wood-block constructions were gleefully demolished by Dorothy whenever they attained fourth-story height.

"Uncle Dring!" Dorothy proclaimed happily when she looked up, abandoning Metoo to rush at the cute alien. Metoo hesitated for a few seconds, as if he was considering flying after her, but then his Stryx building instincts took over. Moving as quickly as the eye could follow, he rapidly built a structure that looked like the central pier of a bridge or a vault, with cantilevered blocks extending in four directions.

Dorothy was torn between trying to convince Dring to tell her a story and the temptation to knock down Metoo's construction. Her four-year-old body quivered for a moment, like a runner waiting for a starter's gun to begin the race. Then she abandoned Dring and ran back to swipe a protruding block from Metoo's masterpiece, leading to a spectacular collapse. Metoo patiently gathered the blocks and began slowly building again.

"Interested in a beer?" Joe asked Dring, with the idea of getting his own empty mug filled without stirring from the couch. "You know where I keep the tapped keg down-stairs. Plenty of clean mugs hanging right above it."

"Thank you, Joe, but I'm just here to swap books. Please tell Kelly that I found 'The Hobbit' to be a fascinating story, though the depiction of Smaug leads me to believe that this Tolkien fellow was biased against dragons," Dring commented. "I think I'll try another Dickens."

"Help yourself," Joe said, gesturing towards the book cases. "I remember reading 'Bleak House' on my first deployment, when I was feeling pretty sorry for myself after losing my family and giving up my home. But Dickens wrote about this orphan boy named Jo, who was so poor that he couldn't even afford a third letter for the name that was his only possession. And I thought, what-ever problems I'm having, at least I'm big enough and healthy enough to look a man in the eye and spell my name with an 'e.' Well, any more and I'll ruin the story for you. It's a good one."

"Thank you for the recommendation. I'll give it a read." Dring hop-skipped his way up the bookshelf, then used his powerful tail as a sort of a living stilt that nearly doubled his reach.

Kelly's indexing system for her library followed the unusual system of putting books in alphabetical order based on the author's first name. She claimed it was a habit from her early days in EarthCent service when she was embarrassed by her inability to remember the first names of her colleagues, and that ordering her books that way had cured the problem.

Dring returned 'The Hobbit' to the Tolkien collection, next to Jane Austen's books, and then he located the Dickens section between Beatrix Potter and Charlotte Bronte. Joe thought it was sad that the Bronte sisters, who had been inseparable in life, were scattered around the shelves by Kelly's system. Kelly maintained that books had lives of their own, and that the sisters were probably enjoying a little breathing space after being stuck next to each other on the same shelf for a couple hundred years. 'Bleak House' turned out to be a battered paperback reprint edition with tiny print, but Dring handled it with reverence.

"Paul tells me you've flown supercargo on a number of Raider runs, and even been out trading with Blythe," Joe said. "You've obviously been around the track a few times. What's so interesting about sitting in a mock-up of a ship and flying around the gameverse shooting stuff, or piling up Trader gold?"

"I've probably been around the track even more times than you can imagine," Dring replied enigmatically. "But this game is something new, something complex. I believe it's worth further study."

"As long as it keeps you camping out in Mac's," Joe replied complacently. "Kelly will be sorry she missed you. She likes talking about books almost as much as reading them."

"Please remind her that she has an open invitation to visit my ship as well," Dring said. He spent another minute watching Dorothy and Metoo locked in their symbiotic cycle of building and destruction, then he turned and trundled out the door.

Joe tapped Beowulf on the nose to try to get the dog to pick up his head, but the wily canine hadn't shown any signs of life since the pretzels ran out. Reluctantly, Joe shifted to bribery and whispered, "Split a beer, boy?"

The old war dog came off the couch like a rocket and headed straight down to the brew room, leaving Joe, whose leg was asleep from the weight of Beowulf's head, to limp after him dangling his empty mug.

Eleven

Kelly was nervous about attending the dinner reception hosted by the Gems, and not because she was worried about the InstaSitter who was watching Dorothy. The Gems were widely reviled as cloners, a technology that most advanced species outlawed early in their development. It didn't help that the Gems had pushed cloning to its logical conclusion, meaning that the whole race consisted of an indeterminately aged woman named Gem, although they did what they could to differentiate themselves in dress, hair style and accessories.

But Kelly was determined to fulfill her mission for EarthCent by taking every opportunity to establish good relations with willing aliens. Joe wasn't too happy when he heard he would be the only male of any kind at the meal, but Kelly assured him that the Gems weren't so much anti-male as psychotically practical.

Libby had briefed Kelly on the history of the Gems, and the story was that they had long ago become so dependent on cloning that they had lost the ability to procreate naturally. At some point, the women who ran the cloning operations had decided to stop cloning men, who after all, were just a nuisance at that point. But eliminating the men turned out to be the beginning of a vicious spiral in which the cloners dropped one individual after the next from their gene pool until there were only two archetypal women left. They fought a raging war for a few thousand years, and then there was only one.

A clone met the human couple at the entrance to the Gem embassy and introduced herself.

"I'm Ambassador Gem," the roughly humanoid woman told them. "Perhaps you had figured that out already. My sisters and I rarely communicate vocally, but we know from experience that species who are dependent on the spoken word find it easier to converse when everybody in the room doesn't share the same name. So please just call me Ambassador, and I'll introduce you to my sisters by their embassy duties."

"Thank you, Ambassador," Kelly replied. "That's very thoughtful of you. I'm Kelly McAllister, and this is my husband, Joe."

"You don't need to state the obvious," Ambassador Gem told her, and escorted them to an intimate dining room with a table set for six. "We will soon be joined by Trade, Military and Propaganda. Cook is preparing Earth foods for you, and if you want anything at all, just tell Waitress."

"Thank you again," Kelly said, hoping that Ambassador Gem wouldn't insist on telling her that no thanks were necessary. She had the feeling that after tens of thousands of years of living with herself, Gem might have purchased an expertise in intrapersonal skills at the expense of being able to communicate with, well, not-Gem. "It's always an honor for us newcomers to be received by elder species."

"Of course," Ambassador Gem agreed. "Now, before I invite the others in, I want to discuss some classified business. Is Joe just your husband, or does he have an official EarthCent position?"

"I'm the Military Attaché to Union Station," Joe replied, using the position Kelly had invented for his upcoming expedition with Jeeves to the staging base on Zach's World. He threw in a stiff bow, and since his evening wear was actually an old dress uniform, he looked quite believable in the role.

"Very good," Ambassador Gem replied. "Trade, Military and Propaganda will be presenting you with their own proposals, but they do not know that I have been given the go-ahead from our highest level, from Premier Gem herself, to make you this offer. If Earth accepts all of our proposals, we will establish a clone line for each of you, as a bonus."

"But I don't want to be cloned!" Kelly exclaimed without thinking. Joe merely looked at the backs of his hands, already waiting for the evening to be over.

"That's ridiculous," Ambassador Gem replied. "Everybody wants to be cloned, at least, everybody that I know. The other species are just jealous of me, of us. I understand you may feel obligated to make this response, in case, for example, this meeting is being bugged by our generous landlords, but the offer stands."

Waving off Kelly's further protests with an exaggerated wink, Ambassador Gem clapped her hands and the doors flew open. Three Gems, each wearing a hand printed English name card identifying them as Trade, Military, and Media, entered the room. Ambassador Gem presented each of them to the humans, but apparently she couldn't read English herself since she introduced Media as Propaganda. Propaganda Gem flinched, and after a brief round of silent communication with Ambassador Gem, through which the message was delivered either by telepathy or by making funny faces, Propaganda Gem spoke.

104

"Please take your seats. I've informed Ambassador that her choice of words may have been open to misinterpretation by your translation devices. We aren't in the habit of using speech amongst ourselves, so please allow for such minor faux-pas."

"We understand, Media," Kelly replied generously, though she was sure that Ambassador Gem was being more truthful than the name card. The four Gems took their places with weirdly synchronized precision, followed by Kelly, for whom her husband, on his best behavior, had reflexively pulled out a chair. This led all of the Gems to bare their teeth, though whether they were communicating with each other or just expressing their views on chivalry wasn't clear.

Waitress Gem brought in a tray with four tall glasses and two pre-packaged meals, with labels from one of the deep space passenger liners that plied the Stryx routes. Joe surreptitiously examined the date code on his meal before peeling back the foil. The Gems each accepted a tall glass full of a viscous, chalky fluid from Waitress Gem, and began to ladle it into their mouths with long handled spoons.

Kelly tried to look pleased as she peeled back the foil from her own chicken dinner with rice, baby carrots, and an unidentifiable spongy thing that was probably somebody's idea of cake. At least Cook Gem had heated it to the proper temperature, and compared to the meal-in-a-glass option, it looked downright gourmet.

"It appears that due to some clerical error on your part, we weren't invited to the recent EarthCent Exposition, at which you granted trade credentials to all attendees," Trade Gem said, after carefully licking off her spoon between swallows. "Will it be necessary to pay you a large bribe to correct this situation?"

Kelly choked on the dry rice and looked around for a glass of water or anything else to wash it down. Joe helpfully thumped her on the back a couple of times, and a few stray grains of rice flew out of her mouth, one of which landed in Military Gem's impeccable black hair.

"Could you get her something to drink?" Joe asked Waitress Gem, who hovered behind them with her empty tray. Waitress Gem fled from the room like she had forgotten to turn off the gas.

Kelly managed a few deep breaths and waved Joe off. "I'm okay, I'm fine. Just went down the wrong way." Then she fished around in her purse and drew out a manila envelope. "I'm glad you understand we didn't mean anything by omitting to send you an invitation for the Exposition. The list was drawn up after we received an unusual volume of requests to attend functions, so we were really just trying to clear the decks."

"And the bribe?" Trade Gem prompted.

"No bribe is necessary," Kelly replied, and extended the envelope. "I brought eight, um, certificates with me. They're identical to the ones I was handing out at the Exposition."

"One would have been sufficient," Trade Gem replied ungraciously. The other Gems cast suspicious looks at Kelly, as if she had offered an intentional insult to their cloning technology by bringing her own copies. Who would have expected the newcomers to be so clever at diplomacy?

Waitress Gem returned in a rush, with a bottle of chilled champagne balanced on her tray, alongside two champagne flutes that kept clinking off each other due to her trembling. She looked visibly upset, and all five Gems fell silent for a moment as if they were working something out among themselves. Then she brought the tray to Military Gem, who removed the bottle and began examining the foil around the neck.

"I can open that," Joe offered, reaching across the table. Military Gem just gave him a cold stare and returned to probing the foil with her sharpened fingernails.

"I have set aside a prime segment on Gem Today to feature the new cooperation between our civilizations," Propaganda Gem announced importantly after polishing off her drink meal. "Since you are newcomers on the galactic stage, I will explain the basic production so that there will be no misunderstandings when you come to our studios tomorrow for the shoot."

"That's very considerate of you, Prop, uh, Media Gem," Kelly replied, wondering if she had missed some small print on the invitation. "However, I'm afraid I wasn't aware of this planned, er, media event, and I don't know if I'll have the time tomorrow."

"You'll make the time when you hear what we're planning," Propaganda Gem asserted. "Gem Today is the one required broadcast for our sisters, guaranteeing you an audience of over thirty billion viewers. I've prepared a list of the protocols for aliens appearing on Gem Today, so before I give it to you to memorize, I'll just read through and test your comprehension."

As Propaganda Gem removed a display sheet from her tunic, Kelly noticed that Joe was holding up both of his hands around shoulder height, palms-out, as if he was thinking halfheartedly about surrendering. Then she realized that his left hand was just in front of his chin, and his right was shaded over to cover her lower face.

"Incoming," he muttered to Kelly under his breath, and she followed his gaze to where Military Gem was struggling with the champagne bottle. The clone had removed the foil and was trying to pry out the cork with her thumbs. The bottom of the bottle was pressed against her upper abdomen and the neck was pointed across the table, sweeping an arc that covered most of the room as she struggled to dislodge the cork. Kelly let herself slip lower in the chair and brought her own right hand up to her forehead, as if she needed to concentrate while listening to Propaganda Gem's list of conditions.

Propaganda Gem began reading her list, pausing briefly after each point. "At no time can your head be higher than that of any Gem on the set. Speak only in response to questions. No clothing or jewelry of any type is permitted on set during production. You will make no mention of so-called 'natural' procreation under any circumstances."

"Wait, hold on a minute," Kelly broke in, as her divided attention caught up with what Propaganda Gem was saying. "Did you say something about being naked?"

"Of course. The whole point of Gem Today is to demonstrate to our sisters the superiority of our system. To allow you to disguise your inferior physical form with clothing on our broadcast would be to perpetrate a fraud on ourselves," Propaganda Gem explained. "Now where was I? Oh yes. When asked about your aspirations for humanity, you will answer that..."

Propaganda Gem got no further as the cork finally popped out of the well-shaken champagne bottle and hit her in the mouth. Stunned, and bleeding from a cut on her lip, she rose from the table and stormed out of the room.

Military Gem was clearly more annoyed about the foam getting on her uniform sleeves than any other collateral damage. She assumed a triumphant expression as she placed the bottle back on the tray, and Waitress Gem immediately brought it around to the other side of the table.

Joe, always mindful of the old rule that you should hold a lady by the waist and a bottle by the neck, filled the two champagne flutes. Both he and Kelly felt a little awkward drinking by themselves, especially after Propaganda Gem had been rendered hors de combat. But any guilt feelings they might have harbored were dispelled by the taste of the champagne, which neither of them touched again after the first sip.

"We are prepared to consider an alliance," Military Gem announced in the aftermath of the uncorking, apparently seeing herself in a position of maximum strength. "Of course, you will agree to operating under our command, and we will supply liaison officers to all of your Raider combat groups. I have drawn up an agreement, which is nonnegotiable, but I'm sure you will be honored to sign."

"Uh, Joe is our military attaché." Kelly passed the buck gladly as she glanced at her decorative wristwatch. The InstaSitter was scheduled to work until midnight, so if they wrapped this up in a hurry, they still had time for a nice evening out.

"Yes, well, I'm a little confused here," Joe admitted. None of the Gems looked surprised at his statement. "You want to establish a military alliance in the gameverse?"

"Exactly," Military Gem replied. "Earth has no organized fleet in real space, since being dependent on the Stryx seems to suit you. But our military intelligence reports that humans have rapidly built one of the most powerful fleets in the gameverse, which is an area where we are, um, not."

"Not?" Joe questioned cautiously. "As in, not present?"

"It's a boring male dominated game," Military Gem burst out. "I could understand if there was something interesting to do, like growing food or taking care of pets, but it's all trading and shooting, trading and shooting. I don't understand the attraction at all!"

"So, why exactly is it you're interested in having a gameverse military presence?" Joe probed gently.

"Everybody else is forming alliances, and we're getting left out again," Military Gem responded bitterly.

Kelly decided it was time to put her diplomatic skills to work. She jerked her head to attract attention, and then held it rigid, staring directly in front of her and moving her eyes, as if reading on her heads-up display. After a few seconds, she announced, "I'm sorry, but something important has come up and we have to leave now. Thank you very much for the dinner and the kind offers of cooperation. I certainly hope we can talk again in the future."

Joe was even faster up out of his seat than Kelly, and the Gems rose in unison to see off their guests. This was probably typical of how their diplomatic dinners drew to a close.

"That offer I made was authorized for a limited time only," Ambassador Gem hinted to Kelly as she escorted the humans to the door.

"Don't feel you have to remind us," Kelly replied. "We'll, uh, call you."

Twelve

"Is it normal for humans to have imaginary friends?" Libby asked over the office speakers. While Donna was certainly on good terms with the station librarian, they weren't close friends like Libby and Kelly, and Donna couldn't recall the last time Libby had initiated a conversation with her.

"Sure, Libby. It's very common at Dorothy's age, even a little later. Are you asking because she talks to an imaginary friend while you are supervising her InstaSitters?" Donna couldn't suppress a flicker of a smile at Kelly's expense.

"No. Dorothy doesn't have an imaginary friend that I've noticed, at least, not one she engages in long conversations."

"She's still a bit young for it, I guess," Donna replied. "Blythe didn't have an imaginary friend, probably because she always had a willing audience in Chastity. But Chastity did have an imaginary little boy she played with when Blythe wasn't around."

"Actually," Libby paused for a moment, "I was thinking of Kelly. She's always talked to herself, usually it's just compliments or insults, but in the last month she's taken to discussing everything from galactic politics to literature with an imaginary friend. Oops, here she comes. Don't say anything," Libby concluded hastily and withdrew.

"Morning, Donna," Kelly greeted her friend and office manager cheerily. "What's new with the wonder girls that has Blythe skipping dates with Paul? The poor boy moped around the house for nearly an hour after she cancelled last night."

"Really? Moped?" Donna asked skeptically.

"Well, maybe he went out to play Raider/Trader, but I'm sure he would have enjoyed it more if she was there," Kelly answered defensively.

"Since you brought it up, did you know the girls expanded InstaSitter to provide incubation services last cycle?"

"Incubation? Like sitting on eggs?"

"Sure. Many of the species on the station are egg-layers, including the Dollnicks," Donna reminded her. "Incubation is a highly stressful time for the Dollys because one of the parents always has to keep the eggs warm, and the girls have hired a whole flock of Dollnick sitters. You haven't seen their ad campaign?"

"No, I guess I missed it," Kelly confessed. She was beginning to wonder if Donna's teenage daughters weren't doing more for interspecies relations with their business than she was with her embassy. "Are they up to anything else?"

"Yes, and it's actually quite brilliant. When you and I got started with EarthCent, it was already a few decades after the Stryx came along and changed everything, but the majority of the human expatriates were still fairly young. It used to be rare that you'd meet somebody past middle age in space. But today, even with all the medical technology, some older humans need quite a bit of help to get by. We don't age as gracefully as the more advanced species."

"Don't tell me. They've expanded into elder care?"

"It's a natural fit. The girls say that the business model is nearly identical to babysitting, though there's a different set of medical challenges. Little kids are a choking risk with swallowing toys, while older people are more likely to choke on—but you aren't really interested in the details," Donna interrupted herself.

"Is Libby still handling all of their bookings and overhead for a cut of the action?" Kelly asked.

"Oh yes. As a matter of fact, Libby asked Gryph to put the girls together with the other first generation Stryx who run stations, and that's why Blythe cancelled last night. It looks like the girls want to franchise InstaSitter throughout the whole station network, but I'm hoping Blythe doesn't spend all of her time traveling. She's only seventeen, after all, and I've told her that Chastity doesn't leave the station on her own until she's seventeen as well. I'm afraid the girls are more sheltered than they realize after growing up in such a safe environment."

"So this meeting with the other first generation Stryx went well?" Kelly couldn't help asking. "They're all going into business together?"

"That's the plan," Donna said with a sigh. "I know I should be happy, but part of being a parent is providing for your children. It's pretty clear at this point that the girls will never need our help again, financially I mean, and Blythe is pretty good at taking care of herself altogether."

Kelly hadn't thought of it that way, and for the first time she felt a wave of sympathy for Donna's position as mother to a brace of overachieving daughters.

"Well, with the Stryx as business partners, I don't imagine you'll ever have to worry about the physical safety of the girls, as long as they don't travel too far off the tunnel

113

network. How is Stan taking all of this?" Kelly asked curiously.

"Stanley? I think he would have left his job to work for the girls by now if not for all the business related to this new game. He doesn't want to leave Fight On in a lurch after they paid our bills for almost twenty years, so he's training a new assistant to take over from him. I think he said the young man is Paul's co-pilot or something when they play together."

Kelly tried for a moment to recall if Paul had introduced her to a copilot, but drew a blank. The truth was that she sympathized with the Gems when it came to Raider/Trader. Nothing about the game held her interest. It had taken her years to develop an appreciation for Nova when Paul was practicing to become a grandmaster. But with Nova, at least you could watch the ebb and flow of the action in the holo cube, and it took on a sort of symphonic feel when the players were masters and evenly matched.

"How am I doing for dinner invitations this week?" Kelly asked, in order to change the subject before she got drowsy. It had become a standing joke around the house that nothing put her to sleep faster than gaming talk, and she occasionally asked Joe to fill her in on Paul's squadron activities when she had a touch of insomnia.

"If this had only happened six years ago, you never would have had all of those money problems because you'd have been eating for free every night," Donna replied.

A chime sounded in Kelly's ear and the message, "Collect call from mother," appeared before her eyes. Kelly sighed and said, "Accept charges," out loud. Donna would understand that Kelly was now talking to her mother, who was probably the last person in the galaxy who knew that calling collect was even possible.

"I can't believe I let you talk me out of space travel for all of those years," her mother began. "The cruise ship put in at Thuri Minor this morning, and it's a paradise. How could you not have invited me to visit when you worked here?"

"I was just a second secretary in a big embassy, Mom. It's the pleasure planets that draw all of the human tourists which end up needing large embassy staffs. I lived in a closet-sized apartment and spent all of my time getting clueless Earthmen released from Thurian jails. There were only three simple rules that the Thurians enforced for tourists: No littering, no public cursing and no cutting in line. I think the government earned enough through court fines that they didn't need tax revenue."

"Well, the first two won't be a problem, but the lines are a bit long," her mom hedged. "Anyway, I checked in with the embassy when we arrived, just to be on the safe side, and it turns out that you're famous here! They invited me to an official reception because I'm your mother, and I'm just coming home from it now. Can you imagine?"

Unfortunately, Kelly could imagine, but even though money was no longer an immediate problem, she didn't want to discuss what her mother had said to the EarthCent staff at collect call rates.

"That's great, Mom. I hope they treated you well. I'm expecting you in another three weeks, right?"

"And I'm looking forward to meeting my scrumptious granddaughter for the first time, but that's not why I called," her mother replied, sounding just a bit hurt that Kelly wasn't interested in a blow-by-blow description of her evening. "I sat next to a Thurian real estate developer at the dinner and he told me about some phenomenal investment opportunities here. I'm going to look at some properties with him tomorrow morning, before the prices go up again. The reason I called was to see if you and Joe have any extra money you want to invest."

"Mother! You can't just show up on a planet and start buying real estate. Thuri Minor is crawling with scammers who make a living selling time-share hotel rooms to tourists who can never afford the time or money to make the trip again. Just because there are a hundred moons in the sky at night and huge forests full of friendly furry animals doesn't mean the real estate prices can go up forever."

"I think I know something about investing, dear," her mother replied. "At least I owned my own house when you needed a loan just to afford someplace to sit."

"LoveU isn't just a chair," Kelly began to argue, but then she cut herself off. "Look, Mom. At least talk to Dad before you do anything big. Alright?"

"Your father is a hundred light years away, standing in a river with freezing water up to his hips and trying to convince a trout to make a meal of an artificial fly. I don't think he's in a position to advise me on Thurian real estate," Kelly's mother replied calmly. "Besides, it's my money, and I'll invest as I see fit. You'll thank me one day when you inherit."

"It's the first stop on your cruise," Kelly changed tack to argue. "Doesn't it make more sense to visit all of the resort worlds on the itinerary so you can make comparisons? You can always buy something on the way home if you want."

"Please, Kelly. You can't spend your life wondering if there will be a better deal tomorrow or you'll never commit to anything. I'm still surprised you didn't let Joe slip through your fingers, though I'm eternally thankful that you didn't."

Kelly was still trying to come up with a new argument when her mother surprised her for the second time in as many months by saying, "Give everybody my love. See you soon," and breaking the connection. Back when Kelly couldn't afford the charges, it had taken a crowbar to end a conversation with her mother. Now it seemed that the situation had reversed.

When she looked up, Kelly found that she had wandered into her office while talking to her mother, and had even sat down at her display desk. There were more consultation requests from humans, which Donna would batch together into a group meeting, and a number of invitations for the EarthCent military attaché. Kelly was beginning to question whether creating the position for her husband had been thought through all the way, but Joe and Jeeves were leaving on their mission today, and maybe Joe would resign when they got back.

"Libby?" she said to the ceiling.

"Yes, Kelly. How can I help you?"

"Do you know anything about real estate frauds on Thuri Minor?"

"If you mean shady operators selling tourists land that isn't theirs to sell, no. The Thurians take their law quite seriously. You should remember that from being posted there."

"I'm just worried that my mother is thinking of investing in some deal there without looking into the details carefully. It's just a two-day stop on a cruise for her."

"Your mother is a mature human and I'm sure she's capable of taking care of her own investments," Libby reassured Kelly. Then she added the mysterious advice,

"Don't let it worry you to the point that you start talking to yourself."

Thirteen

The Nova, carrying one human, one Stryx, and a cargo of four half-kegs of Joe's homebrew, popped into space above Zach's World just seconds after clearing Union Station's core. That's when Joe realized that Jeeves was standing next to him on the bridge, rather than out on the hull where he could have employed one of his Stryx add-ons to boost the ship's propulsion.

"Are you going to tell me how you did that?" Joe asked the robot.

"That?" Jeeves asked innocently. "That was all Gryph. When I told you it would only be a few hours of flight time, I was talking about the way back. Gryph can throw a little ship this size very accurately when it's close to the station. Making the return trip provides a bit of a challenge, because I'll have to get us up to speed and provide a strong beacon for him to lock onto so he can pull us through."

"If I ask you to explain how he does it, are you going to tell me that this is another one of those things that humans lack the brains to understand?" Joe asked, certain that the answer would be one word with three letters. Jeeves surprised him by answering with another question.

"Do you have a basic understanding of how the Stryx tunnel network operates?"

"Not really," Joe admitted.

"At least you're honest," Jeeves replied. "What Gryph did is analogous to creating a single-use tunnel, an unstable solution to a rather complicated set of equations. It requires a tremendous amount of energy to push through, on the order of what a large Stryx station can supply, and it's really very inefficient. But I explained to him that you are doing me a favor, so he agreed."

Joe knew how the Stryx hated inefficient engineering solutions, so he felt properly complimented and let the subject drop. Besides, the surface of Zach's World was rapidly approaching on the main viewer. Typically, appearing in space above a planet would result in an immediate challenge from a ground-based controller. But Zach's World was an open planet with only the loosest government, really just a glorified volunteer search-and-rescue group that monitored the spectrum for local distress calls.

"We're coming around to the staging base and I'm beginning our descent," Jeeves continued. "I expect they'll be hailing us in three, two, one..."

"Attention incoming ship, Nova. Your transponder identifies your homeport as Union Station. State the nature of your business. Over."

"This is Commander McAllister, EarthCent Military Attaché for Union Station," Joe replied, though he felt a little odd about claiming a job title that came without a real job. "I'm accompanied by Stryx Jeeves of Union Station, and we're just coming in for a little look around. Please advise best landing location. Over."

"That's a negative, Nova," the voice replied. "I don't show you on our active roster and this is a closed base, military only. Do not attempt to land. Repeat. Do not attempt to land. Out."

120

Joe looked over at Jeeves, who gave the robotic equivalent of a bored shrug. Time to get serious.

"McAllister to base. I'm carrying beer. Over."

A full minute ticked by while Joe waited for some warning lights or word from Jeeves that they were being targeted. Then a burst of static came over the comm and the main viewer switched into conferencing mode. The scarred face of a man in his early forties came on the screen.

"That you, Joe? How much beer are we talking? Over."

"Wooj. Good to see your ugly face. I'm carrying four barrels of homebrew, best on Union Station. I know because I made it myself. Over."

"Roger that, Nova. You're cleared for landing. Use the small pad just north of the base, and a lorry will be out to meet you. They're turning on the landing lights now. Over and out."

"Was this Wooj one of your men?" Jeeves asked.

"Other way around," Joe replied. "He's a few years younger than me, but he was one of the last guys I knew who was trained in one of the old national militaries, Republic of Korea. Tough, tough soldier, but a good man to follow. Wouldn't throw lives away just to make a show for the client."

A tiny red light appeared out of the darkness on the ground, and slowly resolved into a circle as the ship slowed and descended. A fantastic display of electrical discharges lit up the atmosphere behind the Nova, as the reentry heat, which was converted directly into electricity by the ship's skin, was dissipated. Then the circle of red beacon lights resolved into multiple concentric circles, each blinking on and off in turn, creating the illusion of an expanding bull's eye. Jeeves set the Nova down in the dead center, and without further ado, popped the main hatch.

"I'll just take a quick look around," Jeeves said, and then darted out into the cold wind. It took Joe a moment to figure out that Jeeves was acting in accordance with a promise Kelly had extracted from the Stryx, not to let her husband take any unnecessary risks.

Joe stuck his head outside, noticed that the ladder looked higher than it seemed back on the station, and triggered the hatch mechanism to close. Then he grabbed his gym bag and took the bridge ladder down to the technical deck, where the kegs were stored. Next he hit the hydraulic control to start dropping the main hold door, which doubled as a ramp. He was wrestling the fourth keg into position at the top of the ramp when the lorry appeared and Jeeves arrived back from his recon.

The lorry driver hopped out of his three-wheeler, which reminded Joe of the sort of vehicle one would expect to see utilized for light grounds maintenance work in a park, hauling leaves or grass clippings in its low, short bed. It was painted black, with an emblem that looked like an artist's conception of the perfect spiral arm galaxy, an image that had been used by every unimaginative empire since space flight had been developed. Joe wondered if the equipment had been purchased surplus somewhere.

"Let's go, Beer Man," the young driver called up the ramp. He crouched and clapped his hands like he was waiting to receive a throw. "Roll 'em down."

"You do realize that these kegs are full of beer, not foam?" Joe regarded the young mercenary in amusement. "If I roll one down, it's going right over you, or through you, and maybe through your little truck as well. Are you sure that thing can even take the weight?"

The driver continued to crouch and clapped again, swaying noticeably, and Joe began to suspect that the kid had either drawn the short straw, or been the low man on the totem pole at a party that had been going on for some time. Joe sighed and looked around for the two-wheeled hand truck he had used to load the beer with Paul, hoping he hadn't left it back at Mac's Bones. Fortunately, Jeeves was in an uncharacteristic hurry to get the show on the road.

"Just hop in the cab with the driver," Jeeves instructed Joe, as he floated up and grabbed the top edge of an aluminum keg in each pincer. "I'll load two of these on the kid's tricycle and I'll bring the other two myself. Don't worry about the ship, I'll close up."

"Thanks, Jeeves," Joe replied, and strode down the ramp to the inebriated driver, who was still crouched like a baseball catcher waiting for a pitch. "Let's get in, son. It's cold, and I've always wanted to drive one of these things." Fortunately the kid was used to taking orders, and a few minutes later, Joe was backing the little lorry up to the loading dock of the building that the driver had pointed out as the mess hall, before slumping unresponsive against the door.

Woojin must have been waiting just inside at the window, because the overhead door began to rise before Joe killed the motor and got out. The kid had fallen asleep, so Joe went around to the other side of the cab, opened the door, and caught him as he fell out.

"Inside, son. It's too cold to sleep out here." Joe gave the youngster a push towards the stairs and watched as the kid stumbled up to the dock and through the overhead door.

Woojin was followed outside by four boisterous men in T-shirts, who grabbed a pair of kegs from the lorry and carried them inside like they were hauling ammunition crates, two men per keg. Jeeves floated after them with the other two kegs, and Joe and Woojin brought up the rear. Woojin closed the overhead door and left the kid sleeping in the supply room.

"Not like you to send a boy to do a man's job, Wooj," Joe said to his former superior officer from several deployments.

Pyun Woojin took his time studying Joe's face for information before replying. "I see life has been good to you, Joe. I heard a while back that you stuck it out on Union and even tied the knot. Still got the boy you pulled out of the wreckage on that mining colony?"

"Paul. He's a great kid, but he's eighteen already, so I won't hold him much longer. He won the Nova tourney that the Drazen held a year back. And I taught him everything he knows," Joe boasted.

"You mean you taught him everything you know. He couldn't have won beans if he didn't have more than that going for him," Woojin corrected Joe. "So how does one become an EarthCent military attaché when EarthCent lacks a military?"

"Uh, my wife is the ambassador," Joe admitted.

Woojin stopped, barked a short laugh, and slapped Joe on the back hard enough to make him stagger. "You've got more sense than I gave you credit for, McAllister." Without waiting for an answer, he returned to his line of questioning. "And what's the story with your little robot friend? Strikes me as a bit odd to have a Stryx working as a barback."

Joe vacillated for a second between telling the whole truth and the partial truth, and decided on the latter course even though it meant looking silly. It just made more sense to give out the explanation that was easiest to believe.

"My wife made him promise to keep me out of trouble," Joe replied. "Somehow, she's built up a lot of credit with the Stryx."

"That's a woman I'd like to meet one day. Does she have a sister?" Wooj was having trouble holding back his laughter, and Joe saw that the party really had started a while ago.

"Security seems a bit loose around here," Joe said, an understatement if he had ever heard one. "I know it's just a staging base and that the planet is under Stryx protection in any case, but..."

Woojin cut him off with a gesture as they entered the dining hall. "The business is changing, Joe. We don't even run a separate officer's mess here. It's less of a base and more like being on shore leave with nowhere to go. I don't know what that idiot on the comm was doing, telling you not to land in the first place. Probably just mad that he was stuck in the communications shack."

"Oh, man, I hope you brought a tap," a mournful-looking fellow called to Joe from the improvised bar. "Your robot buddy doesn't seem to have one."

Joe reached in his gym bag and pulled out the vital piece of equipment. Over a hundred men in the packed mess broke into cheers.

"You might want to let those kegs settle for a bit before tapping the first one. We haven't rolled them, but the atmosphere was a bit bouncy," Joe warned, as he handed the tap to a guy with a beer tattooed on his arm.

"Do you want to live forever?" the man asked by way of response. Joe exchanged a glance with Woojin and they both backed away. A minute later, the men around the keg were treated to a beer shower, but after that, it only took a couple cups of foam before the flow ran to dark amber and a fire brigade of cups, mugs and glasses began passing under the stream. The men were disciplined enough to make sure that everybody got a share before allowing seconds. Despite the oversized vessels a few men presented, the initial keg held out long enough to provide a first round for everyone.

"That's some good-tasting beer," Woojin complimented Joe, as he lowered his wide-mouthed canteen and wiped his lips. The captain was the only one who had presented a canteen to the tap boss for filling, so Joe figured it meant that officers still had some prerogatives. Either that or Woojin was the only one who thought far enough ahead to return to his quarters and snag a canteen. Meticulous planning had always been one of the things that gave him an edge over the officers who lacked his military college training.

"Thanks," Joe said, relaxing back on the folding chair and hoping it was stronger than it looked. "I've been selling it to a few pubs on the station for the last year or so. Helps to keep me busy."

"Did you already give up on that junk business I heard you won?" Woojin asked. "I figured you'd be good at it, since you always liked fooling around with tools and equipment."

Joe snorted and took a deep sip from his cup. "It's this Raider/Trader game that put me out of the scrap business. First, the players bought up every ship controller and all the bridge hardware I had in order to build mock-ups.

Then we started renting the empty space so the kids would have somewhere to put the things, added shells, and even some full ships. Last count, there were nearly three hundred gamers parked in my hold, all paying rent. And they've formed into a squadron with Paul as the leader. Can you believe that?"

"If he won a Drazen Nova tournament, he's got the makings of a gameverse admiral," Woojin replied. "War games used to be a big part of our training back on Earth, though we played them out on the field with real men and equipment. This new game has some of those elements, and I can tell you I've lost some of the young guys to it already."

"Lost them? You mean you can't get them out of their mock-ups for drill?" Joe asked in amusement. A cheer went up from the men as the second keg was tapped, and Joe looked enviously at Woojin's canteen.

"Lost them as in they left. Some of the kids even skipped out on contracts and forfeited the holdback money. I wouldn't be surprised if you have a couple of them in your barn, playing for Trader gold and selling it on that exchange they all use."

"That's something," Joe replied in wonder. "I knew the game was big, but I didn't realize guys were changing careers for it."

"Fighting for money was never much of a career to start with, and you obviously figured that out before I did," Woojin remarked. "Listen, Joe. What are you really here for? I can see from halfway across the mess that your Stryx friend is pumping the men like they're pumping your kegs. We've got nothing to hide from Big Brother around here, but I tell you, if he starts a poker game, I'm going to have to ask him to leave."

"There have been some weird things going on with Earth, and the Stryx take an interest. You told me yourself that the business is changing. What's with the galaxy symbol on your uniforms? I keep hearing about some consortium taking over the mercenary business and then paying you to sit around and drink beer. If that's the deal, maybe I'll get back in!"

Woojin looked at Joe a little sadly. "No, you're out for good unless somebody comes after that home you've built for yourself. You can tell a man's done with this game just by looking at him, though I guess you've forgotten that." Woojin stopped and took a long, slow pull from his canteen, then weighed it in his hand, as if he was trying to decide if he should make a move now or wait for the third keg to be tapped. A hundred thirsty men make quick work of fifteen gallons of beer.

"I'll tell you what I know because nobody has told me not to," Woojin continued. "The consortium that bought up all of our contracts isn't interested in the old business. They brokered a few deals in the first couple months, but I think that was just to keep the men busy while they got organized, found the right ships, set up some staging bases like this one. At this point, it's clear that they could care less about all the little wars of succession and tech-ban planets that used to pay the bills."

"You mentioned finding ships. Does it mean that it's all fleet actions now?" Joe prompted in a confidential tone.

"Exactly wrong as usual, McAllister," Woojin replied with a laugh. "If I had to sum it up in two words, I'd say that they've turned the whole lot of us into caravan guards. Funny thing is that it's fairly interesting work, lots of planning involved. But in some cases, I've got almost no information to go on. Our last job was escorting a string of

128

jump freighters to a world I can't even pronounce in an area so far off the tunnel network that all their ships have jump drives, though they still used Stryxnet controllers. It took three weeks just to do the round trip."

"Who were the merchants willing to pay for an escort?" Joe asked. "I thought that the high-risk boys always flew armed and were only one bad trade away from becoming pirates themselves."

"My guess is that the folks supplying the caravan guards are the same as the folks who are running the caravans. Just one big happy consortium," Woojin concluded, and tipping up his canteen, drained whatever was left. He let out a happy belch. "Come on, they're tapping the third keg. Let's get back in line before it's all gone."

"What kind of cargo is worth all this fuss? I mean, interstellar trading in this galaxy has been going on for tens of millions of years." Joe tried to think it through as they waited behind a dozen serious drinkers who were getting back in line immediately after their cups were filled and drinking standing up. "I guess I can see the point of hiring guards if you're taking a whole string of jump ships off the tunnel network, but I didn't realize that anybody was that desperate to find new markets."

"This you'll never believe," Woojin said, and put a hand on Joe's shoulder to turn him so they were face to face. "The three-week jaunt I mentioned, to a world so out of it that I didn't recognize the aliens and the traders did some of their bartering in sign language? The ships we were escorting carried a half a million pairs of rubber boots made for Verlocks, twenty thousand empty fire extinguishers from Earth and three thousand barrels of some purple slime being transshipped from nobody knew where."

"Three-toed rubber boots, empty fire extinguishers and purple slime? Sounds more like a practical joke than a trade."

Woojin shrugged and handed his canteen to the tap man for filling. "The merchants all seemed happy. And the stuff they loaded for the return trip? I don't have a clue what most of it was, and I'm not sure anybody else knew much about it either. But they were all in a hurry to get back and unload the stuff on markets because they were working on a tight timetable."

Joe handed his glass over for a refill, feeling a little silly about queuing up for his own beer, but happy there was still enough left for at least one more glass. He wondered how Jeeves was doing with his investigation, especially since Joe couldn't see any deep, dark motive behind what Woojin was telling him.

"Since when do caravans run on a tight schedule?" Joe asked, as they headed back to their table. The other drinkers were leaving them alone, either out of respect for Woojin, or because they were afraid Joe was going to surprise them with a bar bill.

"I guess you came close enough to guessing that I can give you the final piece of the puzzle, but you owe me dinner if I ever make it to Union."

"Deal," Joe replied, and the two men bumped fists in the traditional mercenary oath.

"The merchants weren't independents, they were on commission. That's why I said this consortium is one big happy family." Woojin thumped his chest where the galaxy symbol was sewn on his uniform. "I've been around plenty of markets in my life, you have too. Sure, there was a little give and take between our merchants and theirs, but it was weirdly efficient, like the whole thing had been worked out ahead of time, and we were all just some kind of biological robots making the clockwork turn."

Biological robots. The phrase stuck in Joe's head even after the rest of the evening got fuzzy, thanks to Woojin digging out an old bottle of scotch and insisting they drink each other toasts, Korean style. The last thing he remembered was Jeeves lugging the empty kegs back to the Nova as the men serenaded the robot with dirty limericks that all started, "There once was a girl named Stryx..."

When Joe woke up with his first hangover since before his marriage, they were already approaching the station. He checked his shoulder bag and discovered that the omniscient Stryx had forgotten to bring the tap.

Fourteen

Kelly had never visited any of the Frunge decks on the station before, and Joe told her she was in for a surprise. When they first exited the lift tube, Kelly thought there had been a mistake, and they were arriving on an ag deck set up as a Grenouthian warren for the giant bunnies. Then the rows of bushes burst into activity, and she saw that they were actually Frunge kids playing a slow-motion version of freeze tag, or some similar game.

"I've been reading up on the Frunge," she told Joe, as they picked their way through the mob of children, following a brown pebbled path that led straight away from the lift. The dinner invitation from the Frunge ambassador had enclosed a hand-drawn map on parchment that might have appeared in a children's book. The map included brown paths, round green treetops, and a red X, which indicated either the ambassador's residence or buried treasure. "The children don't get their first hair cut until they come of age. Supposedly, the tradition extends back to their pre-history when blending in with the vegetation helped keep them safe from predators."

"What if the predators were herbivores?" Joe objected, which struck Kelly as a rather good point.

"I didn't get that far," she confessed. "It wasn't really that interesting of a book. The author was obsessed with genetics and cross-breeding, and a lot of technical stuff about soil nutrients. But I'll bet you didn't know that in times of famine, the Frunge can still take root through their feet and get by on nothing but water and photosynthesis."

"I can't say it's ever come up," her husband replied, as they took a side branch off the main path immediately after a large rock that looked like a fake prop from an old science fiction movie. "Did your book have anything about dinner etiquette?"

"No. I even asked Libby to check for a tourist's guide to any of the Frunge worlds, but she said they discourage outsiders from visiting them at home. I know from Shaina and my visits to the Shuk that their biggest export items are blade weapons and wing sets. Kind of weird for a tree-like species, don't you think?"

"I tried those wings on shore leave when I was still young and stupid," Joe replied. "They're kind of great if you aren't afraid of heights, which I am. And I owned a Frunge cavalry saber for a number of years, bought it in one of the Vergallian systems. I can't imagine a Frunge flying with wings or riding a horse into battle, so I guess some ambitious shrub just got into the business a long time ago, and it caught on with them for some reason."

"This must be it," Kelly announced, consulting the map as they arrived at an elegant structure that blended in perfectly with its surroundings. The corner posts of the house looked like living trees, and in place of walls, there were rows of vines trained on strings suspended from above. No door was visible, but when the humans approached along the plainly marked path, a section of the wall vines parted with a gentle rustling sound.

"Welcome to my garden. I am Ambassador Czeros," announced the Frunge who had apparently been waiting for their arrival, or perhaps the living house had informed him of their approach. Then the Frunge ambassador ritualistically bowed in the direction of each corner of the house, reciting a long formula that was translated, "My ancestors also extend their greetings to our visitors from Earth."

Kelly nudged Joe, and together they recited the formula Shaina had taught her. "May the rains nourish your seedlings, may the sun harden their bark."

"How nice of you to say so," the Ambassador replied, sounding genuinely pleased. "Of course, we have neither rain nor sun here, and the children you no doubt saw playing were germinated on one of our worlds, but small matter. It's the sentiment that counts."

"And it's a human tradition to bring a bottle of wine to dinner," Kelly said. After the Gem champagne fiasco, Joe had convinced Kelly that they better start bringing their own drinks to diplomatic events. She motioned to Joe to present the ambassador with a gift bag containing one of the more expensive vintages from the best wine store in the human section. "I couldn't find out from anybody whether or not you drink beverages with alcohol, so I hope it doesn't offend you."

A screeching groan came from the four corners of the house simultaneously, like a branch ripping away from a tree in a storm. Czeros cringed and immediately went to each of the corners, murmuring words of conciliation. Kelly began to suspect that rather than being representative of his ancestors, the corner posts were his direct forbears. The Frunge ambassador returned to the center of the room looking a bit shaken, by which time Joe had wisely wrapped up the gift in his jacket.

"I'm very sorry about this," Czeros apologized. "Cultural misunderstandings will happen, and my ancestors are traditionalists. I, myself, have no qualms about handling, you know, in the course of my duties at the embassy, but I would never bring it home. Please follow me out to the veranda where our dinner is waiting. It is the Frunge custom not to eat within our homes," he concluded, with a significant nod to the nearest living corner post.

"Did you get what all of that was about?" Kelly whispered to Joe, as they followed the ambassador out of a fresh opening at the back of the room.

"I'm betting the old trees are offended by paper bags," Joe whispered back. "Imagine if you were an old horse and somebody brought you glue. Come to think of it, if you took root when you got old and had to live off of artificial light, fertilizer and drip irrigation, you might not be in the mood to watch anybody eating real food, either."

There was a metal table on the veranda with two plastic chairs for the humans, since the Frunge always ate while standing. The ambassador introduced Kelly and Joe to his family, all of whom gave polite acknowledgement, but none of whom appeared to be very interested in the humans. Czeros took his place directly across from Joe, and then he said something which the implants translated as, "Little shrubs have big ears and old logs have sharp eyes." Then he pantomimed unwrapping an invisible package and removing something from within.

Kelly and Joe watched the performance with rapt attention without getting the point. The Frunge ambassador looked up at the ceiling for a moment, then holding an invisible tube firmly in one hand, began twisting an invisible screw into the hollow space with the other.

"Got it," Joe said, and began furtively moving his hand inside the bundle he had made of his jacket and the gift bag. When there was a slight crinkling sound and all heads

135

pivoted in his direction, he whispered to Kelly, "Cover me."

"I've been looking forward to this evening very much," Kelly proclaimed loudly, as Joe extracted the bottle and handed it to their host. "I hope it marks the beginnings of better understanding between our peoples."

"Ah, an excellent year," Czeros remarked, examining the bottle. "You know, we may have more in common than you think. My staff informs me that you have been allying yourselves with those treacherous Drazens, but I can assure you that they have no appreciation for fine wine. In fact, I've heard they purchase our irrigation run-off from the Stryx to use in a fermented beverage."

The Frunge children made some disturbing noises at this statement, and the ambassador's wife said, "Please, Czeros. Don't talk about such things at the dinner table. You'll ruin our appetites."

"Speaking of dinner, where are those confoundedly slow servers with our food?" the Frunge ambassador's voice rose to a shout. "And hurry with those glasses and a bottle opener so I can remove this SYNTHETIC CORK!" Joe and Kelly got the message and exchanged winks.

A rather dignified looking Frunge appeared, bearing a small tray with four glasses, a bottle opener, and a bottle of human wine from the ambassador's private collection. He was quickly followed by another Frunge, wearing some sort of livery, and bearing a silver platter of what looked like raw meat.

"Vat grown," the Frunge ambassador assured Kelly, having caught her expression. "Don't worry, we prepared something special for you. My butler said there was a minor problem with the order but it will be out in a minute."

"Please don't wait for us," Kelly said graciously, since the young Frunge were plainly fixated on the silver platter with its mound of meat.

"Thank you," Czeros said, giving his family the go-ahead to begin. He opened the wine bottle Joe had presented, filled four glasses, and passed two across the table. When Kelly, Joe, and his wife all had glasses, the Frunge ambassador toasted them, "May your sap flow quickly."

"Bottoms up," Joe replied, assuming the toast required a response, but not willing to gamble on a horticultural shot in the dark.

The butler reappeared and started a whispered conversation with the ambassador, while the second Frunge deposited another silver tray on the table in front of Kelly and Joe. The food bore a ghostly resemblance to the take-out banquet they'd been served at the Drazen ambassador's home, except it looked they were only getting bits and pieces that had been recovered from the garbage. Kelly was surreptitiously examining a broken hamburger patty for bite marks, and Joe was prodding at what appeared to be a mound of pizza toppings, when the Frunge ambassador finished conferring with the butler and hastened to explain.

"I'm told that on your Earth there is a competition for uninhabited land between the, er, trees and the grasses. Is this translating correctly? On the Frunge home world, there was a similar competition in our ancient past which was settled by a mutual non-aggression pact. Although we Frunge evolved into the dominant species, we honor the memory of our ancestors through abiding by the spirit of the pact. I hope you understand," Czeros concluded awkwardly, then helped himself to a piece of raw meat from the rapidly diminishing pile that was feeding his family.

"No grasses?" Joe murmured to Kelly out of the side of his mouth.

"No grains. That's sushi," she mouthed back, pointing sadly at a series of little heaps on the tray that now resolved into sushi rolls, with every grain of rice stripped away. Along with bunless burgers, crustless pizza and a puddle of watery tomato sauce that looked like it had been rinsed off of spaghetti, the entire meal that had been sanitized of cereal crops. Joe stopped hoping that beer would appear on the menu and began to eat.

"I should have brought our daughter," Kelly said brightly, as she tried to cut into a burger with her fork. "She's only four and she hates eating the, uh, you-know-what part of the pizza. I'm sure she would have enjoyed meeting your children. We see so few Frunge in the human sections, just in the Shuk."

"Yes," Czeros said noncommittally. Then he jabbed the last piece of meat on the Frunge platter with his fork, yanking it out of harm's way as the implements of his voracious offspring stabbed at empty air. The children quickly asked to be excused, which was granted, and the Frunge ambassador's wife apologized for not feeling well and followed them out. So the dinner company was reduced to Czeros and the two humans.

"I hope we haven't made your family uncomfortable, Ambassador Czeros," Kelly ventured. "We professional diplomats sometimes forget that the very sight or smell of each other can be difficult for those who aren't accustomed to inter-species contacts."

"Please call me Czeros," the Frunge ambassador replied, and then belched contentedly. "My people and my family are far too provincial, and this living in the constant presence of our ancestors has long been a serious brake on our progress. For example, would you believe that we're one of the few species on the station that doesn't use InstaSitter? The ancestors refuse to countenance it, and since we have no tradition of babysitters, I have to sit at home every night or be the bad guy for abandoning my wife to do all of the work. This is the first time I've ever invited anybody here, and you can see how well that worked out." He wrapped up his plaintive speech with a gesture at the mangled remains of the take-out food.

"Oh, we really appreciate all of the trouble you took," Kelly protested mechanically. "I'm sure some hosts would have thrown it all away and just offered up what you were having."

Czeros barely seemed to be listening to Kelly as he re-filled Joe's wine glass, and then tossed off the untouched contents of his wife's glass. He gave himself another refill and continued mournfully.

"I thought that working my way up to ambassador was the way out, a chance to see the galaxy. I should have become a trader," he groaned, drained his glass, and reached for the corkscrew and the second bottle of wine.

Kelly kicked Joe under the table and made the universal "drink up" gesture at him. A half a bottle of wine more or less had little impact on Joe, so she wanted him to keep pace with the Frunge. If Kelly had been a spy, seeing the Frunge load up on alcohol might have fit her plans. But she was hoping to have an intelligent discussion with the alien, not to sit and listen to drunken recitations of broken dreams.

"Was there anything in particular you wanted to dis-cuss when you invited us?" Kelly prompted Czeros, in hopes it wasn't too late to salvage some diplomatic gains from the evening. The Frunge had finally succeeded in messily uncorking the second bottle, and as he poured himself and Joe another glass, Kelly could see from the stray crumbs floating in the wine that the cork had been natural wood.

"Trade treaty, military treaty, blah, blah, blah," Czeros reeled off pathetically. "More money? More bragging rights?" He gave his chest a thump so hard that it rustled his vine-like hair, and then he lowered his voice to a mournful whisper. "I don't know what I'm doing here. Give me half a reason and I'd defect to anybody but the Drazens."

"It can't be that bad," Kelly began, but Joe poked her arm to get her attention, and drew a finger across his throat to cut her off. She was going to ignore him and continue anyway, but then she saw that the Frunge ambassador had tipped the bottle up to his mouth, and whatever he wasn't chugging was running down the bark of his chin. Still looking significantly at Kelly, Joe tapped his left wrist with his right forefinger.

"I could have been a singer," Czeros announced wretchedly, tossing the empty bottle blindly behind him, where it clunked loudly off one of his ancestors. "But no, I had to maintain the family honor. Honor!" He sobbed out the word.

"Well, we really have to be going," Kelly rose, putting on her best professional smile. "Thank you for the lovely dinner, and I hope we see you again soon."

"Thanks," Joe added, and grabbing Kelly's elbow, steered her rapidly back through the house with its living walls and half-dead ancestors. Behind them there was a loud screeching, which might have been the ambassador beginning to sing, or perhaps he was receiving a scolding. The broken bits of translation didn't make it clear.

"I've seen guys like him a thousand times," Joe told Kelly, as they hurried down the path back to the lift as fast as dignity would allow. "I thought it was a little funny that his family and staff disappeared so fast. Perfect gentleman until he gets to the third glass, then, pow!"

"Do you think he was serious about wanting to defect?" Kelly asked reflectively.

"Sure," Joe replied. "At least at that moment. But really, who would want him?"

Fifteen

"Well, this is rather boring, isn't it?" Blythe remarked, as she pouted at the main viewer. The two enormous fleets were arranged in virtual space like a pair of thin, opposing discs. It was the biggest Raider/Trader battle ever, with tens of thousands of players on each side, and more arriving by the second. The two largest bodies of ships were from Earth and Horten, making them the purported opponents, but each side was now accompanied by more allied ships than the main bodies contained.

"It's getting out of control," Paul admitted. Human-piloted vessels kept reporting in to Patches, who had taken over direct control of the Mac's Bones squadron since Paul had been elevated to an Earth fleet wing commander. Blythe was filling in as the weapons officer in order to earn the combat credit for her game profile, but she didn't see the point of wasting virtual ammunition that would need to be replaced. Most of the participants on both sides agreed with her, so the standoff was largely static, with a few rich boys skirmishing around the edges.

"What are you going to do when the numbers reach the hundreds of thousands, or the millions?" Dring inquired unhelpfully. "I've spent a bit of time studying military developments over the years, and your game is clearly diverging from the natural evolution of force, which always leads to the construction of ever larger and more powerful ships. But what motivation do gamers have to invest their Trader gold in developing capital ships when there can only be one captain?"

"You've got a point," Paul sighed. His eyes never stopped sweeping the opposing wall of ships for a weak point, but the formation may as well have been a giant wet blanket. Reserves clumped behind the front lines and shadowed the movements of the opposing reserves to keep the forces in balance and new ships kept arriving on both sides. "Players are willing to put their ships under the control of a squadron commander or a fleet officer, that's been clear for months. But I've never heard of more than five players adding their Trader gold together to build up a single vessel."

"And in the real universe, capital vessels are generally financed by governments or trading guilds," Dring continued his lecture. "So the financial support for a ship with a crew of a thousand may be paid for by a million, or a ship with a crew of a million may be paid for by a billion. Why, some people would call Union Station itself a capital ship, with this Stryx fellow Gryph in charge, and over a hundred million crew."

"I can't take another four hours of this," Blythe said fiercely and turned to Paul. "You're the Nova battle master or whatever it's called. Do something!"

"Nova is a two-player game," Paul objected. "One wins, one loses. In Nova, I'd force the action by launching a point attack, and then try to outthink and outmaneuver my opponent once things got messy. But I can't just order my wing to make a suicidal attack that I know will cost at least a quarter of the players their ships, even if the rest of our fleet and allies do support the move properly, which is doubtful. It would put all those guys back at square one, rebuilding their game profiles."

"Shout from our invisible overlords on algo channel alpha. It's square," Patches broke into the conversation. "Says, whoa!"

"As in, slow down?" Blythe asked skeptically, as she eyed the lack of action on main viewer.

"It says the opposite," Patches reported, forgetting to speak in banter. "It says that no combat credit will be granted for ships involved in fleet actions unless one side takes over ten percent casualties, effective immediately. And it says that player profiles won't be wiped for ship destruction in fleet actions. They've removed the cost of getting killed!"

"I believe you'll get your excitement now," Dring told Blythe drily.

"Keep the squadron together," Paul shouted at Patches. The main view screen showed the two opposing fleets accelerating towards each other at maximum speed. "Blythe, don't shoot any of our guys." With that, Paul retreated into a world of fevered gibberish consisting of number and color codes, as he coordinated with the other wing commanders in the Earth fleet, and managed the three squadrons under his direct control.

Blythe put her faith in the identification-friend-or-foe system, which in accordance with her preloaded preferences, showed the enemy ships as little green dresses. She kept the weapons hot, taking them up to ninety percent capacity over and over when high probability targets presented themselves, but holding out the last ten percent in case of emergency.

Dring watched with fascination as the commanders on both sides of the battle developed new tactics in real-time.

Discipline broke down almost immediately in the newer squadrons and in some of the ad hoc groupings that were formed from allied ships, creating a background soup of every man for himself. But the older squadrons held together, and began forming a variety of three-dimensional formations that had been practiced and used in smaller fleet actions.

Less than an hour into the battle, the number of participating ships had been reduced to a shadow of the original fleets, with perhaps one in ten remaining. Paul's wing had lost around a quarter of its original ships, but with the "death" of another Earth wing commander, it had grown in size by integrating the two surviving squadrons from the leaderless wing. His reputation as a Nova champion was proving to be a bigger draw for gamers than the recently established chain of command.

Three hours into the battle, both Paul and Patches were hoarse from shouting orders, but the squadron was still operational and had become the rallying point for the remaining Earth ships and their allies. Both fleets were down to a few thousand vessels at this point and had spontaneously disengaged, as if by mutual consent. Paul had the Earth vessels arranged in a formation like a bowl with the base facing the enemy, while the Horten-anchored fleet resembled a starfish with the arms reaching forward. The lone wolves and smaller groupings were all gone. None of them could stand for a second against the concentrated firepower of a large formation.

"Just about an hour left on the clock," Blythe informed them cheerily. "This has been fun, but all the shooting is getting a little monotonous, plus it's making me hungry."

"We can take 'em," Patches croaked to Paul. "That starfish-looking thing is crazy. We could run right in there and take the arms off one by one. It's almost like they're begging us to flank them."

"It's just attrition at this point," Paul rasped in response. "Their remaining ships are the ones with disciplined pilots, same as ours. It's a draw unless somebody does something stupid. It's just a question of how many ships each side will have left at that point."

"You'll think of something," Patches insisted. "We just have to mix it up!"

"It's too even," Paul repeated. "In Nova, I could play to the other guy's personality and style, sacrifice to distract his attention from a weak point and attack. But here he's got thousands of pairs of eyes watching for him, and I'm not going to trick them all."

"Might I ask something?" Dring spoke up for the first time in hours and turned to Patches. "Did the communication from the game programmers you reported earlier contain any other rule changes, or was it just the two you mentioned?"

"There was a bunch of other stuff," Patches replied tiredly. "I just told you the bits that mattered for right now."

"What sort of other stuff?" Blythe asked. "Can I see the transmission?" Patches acquiesced silently and made a few motions in his holo controller. A dense text document appeared on Blythe's jury-rigged fire control station.

"Did you know about this ahead of time, Dring?" Blythe asked suspiciously, looking up from the new addendum to the Raider/Trader rules. "It addresses exactly what you were talking about earlier, the construction of capital ships. It even gives a list of ready-to-go battleships that you can purchase with Trader gold. And players can now get their combat credit by owning a share in a capital ship, they don't have to put in the gameverse time themselves. That's a relief."

"It all sounds logical to me," Dring replied. "No, I didn't know anything about this ahead of time, but the circumstances seemed to demand it. Apparently, the game programmers anticipated the 'fleets of equals' problem, prepared these rule changes as a solution, and then waited to see if their prediction was accurate before making the announcement."

"These pre-built solutions are expensive, but they look pretty neat," Blythe said, as she moved from the text document to the newly-launched gameverse store. "You can buy a Thark battle cruiser for a half a million in Trader gold. But I thought the Tharks were a race of glorified accountants."

"They were an aggressively expanding species that stayed off the Stryx tunnel network until an internal war of succession nearly drove them to extinction," Dring explained. "It's a common problem with warrior cultures when they run out of external enemies or simply fall into schism. The surviving Tharks stumbled into their current role as business enforcers by chance, and the generations have mellowed them. What other ships are featured?"

"It's funny," Blythe answered. "I don't see anything from the species with real navies, like the Drazens or Hortens. It's all aliens I've never heard of before. What's a Brupt Destroyer Sphere? They want a million two for that one."

"The Brupt were very ugly customers," Dring assured her. "I believe the Stryx gave the Brupt a choice between leaving the galaxy and giving up all of their military capabilities. The Brupt chose to leave. Whoever these game programmers are, they either have very long memories or access to an excellent archive."

"The Stryx made them leave?" Paul asked hoarsely, keeping an ever watchful eye on the main viewer, where the opposing fleets continued to drift apart. In another few minutes there would barely be enough time left in the gameverse to reengage if they wanted to. "Since when do the Stryx give anybody orders? I thought they were strictly into soft power."

"Not everybody is amenable to economic inducements or technological bribes," Dring explained. "There have been many occasions where the Stryx have acted to protect their version of the status quo. Whenever a native-grown species or an invader from outside of the Stryx volume of influence has displayed the capability and willingness to conquer or destroy worlds that have joined the tunnel network, the Stryx have presented similar ultimatums."

"But they don't have a military!" Paul argued. "Sure, they have a technological advantage over every other species we know of, but what good is a lab against weapons that can destabilize stars?"

"I see the Stryx must be growing modest in their old age if you, who grew up with them, question their military capabilities," Dring commented dryly. "The Stryx don't need ships and weapons because they ARE ships and weapons. It's their mastery of space and energy that makes them the most powerful of the galaxy's denizens. Perhaps one day another life form will arise that could challenge the Stryx on an even level, but I can't conceive of anything that could defeat them, other than a change in the laws of nature."

"How do you know all of this, Dring?" Blythe asked. She watched him carefully for a reaction, as if she could read something from the face of a small dinosaur.

"I have spent most of my life studying the galaxy and other complex systems. True complexity can only be understood through history, not by looking at the present state of some seemingly complicated construct. If you freeze time, everything becomes simple, or at least, amenable to explanation," Dring corrected himself. "But true complexity encompasses processes, growth, the collisions between objects and peoples, whether they bounce apart, come together, or destroy one another. This gameverse we are currently part of aspires to true complexity by mimicking the real universe."

"When people start making speeches like that, the fighting is over for the day," Patches grumbled. "Should I tell the squadron you're calling it, or are you going to let us just drift away from the Hortens until it's obvious to everybody?"

"Drifting apart works," Paul replied. "It's not like a real war where we'd have casualties to tend or repairs to make. Besides, if I announced the end of hostilities, these gameverse programmers who never had anything to say before today might cancel the last hour's combat credit, or make up a new rule."

"Hey. Do you want a battleship, Paul?" Blythe asked.

"It's a bit late for a birthday present," he mumbled. It had only recently dawned on him that his girlfriend was on her way to becoming seriously rich, and he wasn't sure how he felt about it.

"I'm thinking of it as a business investment," Blythe replied, with the growing enthusiasm that she brought to each new project. "I bet a lot of players would rather invest

149

some Trader gold to buy a share of a capital ship, than to put in the gameverse combat time and have to deal with being a part of a fleet. Most of the gamers I've talked to outside of your barn are playing for the roving trader experience. They view the whole fighting thing as a sort of a tax."

"I'll take a battleship if he won't," Patches offered helpfully. "I already work for your dad, so I may as well work for his daughters."

"You can both have battleships. Listen. I'll use Stryx creds to buy Trader gold on the exchange, and we'll build a fleet quickly. We'll sell shares to whoever wants to get their combat credit without fighting, or maybe offer a discount for qualified players who help crew for battles." Blythe spoke rapidly, making it up as she went along.

"Why wouldn't players just pool their own Trader gold to buy ships?" Paul objected.

"In order to afford and equip one of these virtual pre-builts, it will take thousands of players pooling their Trader gold, and then they won't have it for trading. It's just like the real world. If you tie up all of your capital in an investment without a liquid market, you may as well be broke. And how are thousands of players going to decide on who's in charge of the ship, coordinate buying virtual supplies, and strategize with larger groups? It's why backwards planets like Earth have corporations. They aren't a good solution for anybody other than the executives and the major shareholders who get to make the decisions, but we don't have the alternative business structures in place for large investments."

"So how will this be different from an Earth corporation?" Paul asked stubbornly.

"It won't, but we'll be the executives and the major shareholders," she explained, with a pitying look for his thick-headedness. "I'll bet you dinner at the Burger Bar that all of the other species do the same thing, but with family, guild or clan money instead of a corporation. I wouldn't be surprised if a few governments get involved as well."

"Like I said, I'm in," Patches repeated.

"What are you going to call it?" Paul asked grudgingly.

"InstaNavy," Blythe responded immediately.

Sixteen

"Don't the Verlocks hate everybody?" Joe asked, tightening his grip on the neck of the wine bottle as they exited the lift tube. Thanks to Kelly's lengthy cross-examination of the latest Drazen girl sent out by InstaSitter, they were also running late for the reception. "Are you sure the invitation wasn't a mistake?"

"Is my big, strong, military attaché worried?" Kelly cooed in response, patting his arm. She had already asked Donna to check with the Verlock embassy twice to make sure they were invited, and then she had triple-checked with Libby. "Don't worry, we won't be the only soft-skins there. If the three-toes decide to start eating diplomats, I'm sure they'll start with the Grenouthians. I know I would."

Along with their indifference to other biologicals, the Verlocks were primarily known for their mathematical achievements and their thick, scaly skin. They came from a volcanically active home world, and thanks to seeking out similar worlds when they achieved interstellar flight, they had never come into conflict with other species over colonization rights. The Verlocks could withstand huge temperature swings and breathe a wider range of atmospheres than any of the other unaltered biologicals, but they moved ponderously and spoke like slow-flowing lava.

"Welcome," the Verlock doorman rumbled, starting on the word when the humans were five steps from the door and completing it as they entered the embassy. The reception room was brightly, almost painfully lit, and for the first time Kelly felt jealous of the financial resources of the Natural League members. While it was true that the Stryx supported EarthCent in ways that were beyond a price, there was something to be said for having enough money to build a home away from home.

Behind a wall of tinted glass, lava flowed down a rocky chute into a glowing pool, from which it was continually pumped back up to the top. The floor of the room was tiled in obsidian that glowed with an inner light, perhaps a trick done with lasers. Dozens of artworks created from molten rocks or metals were scattered throughout the space. Some of these constructions may have been intended for utilitarian duties as tables or benches, but Kelly was afraid to be the first to put them to the test.

Ambassadors from many of the other humanoid and vaguely humanoid species were already milling about, most of them holding beverages of some sort or another, which led Joe to start looking for the bar. But just when he located it, aided by the creaking of the Frunge ambassador who had obviously arrived early, the doors to the banquet hall swung open and a bone-rattling gong was struck.

"Dinner is served," intoned the Verlock majordomo, and the crowd of diplomats surged into the dining hall. It was no less splendid than the reception room, with an enormous table that looked like it was carved from a single rock, laid with gold cutlery and other accoutrements suitable for guests from dozens of different species. Holographic place cards floated over each setting, making it easy for the diplomats to locate their places, which were sensibly arranged to avoid violent outbreaks during the meal. It was apparent that when the Verlocks set out to be hospitable, they did so with the maximum effort.

Kelly found herself seated with the Drazen ambassador to her right and Joe to her left. Immediately next to Joe sat a stunning Vergallian woman who was unattended, leaving Kelly to assume she was the ambassador. As the table filled up, all of the diplomats looked around, trying to determine who had been left out. It reminded Kelly of Joe's rule about playing poker, that if you can't spot the sucker at the table, it's you.

Bork, the Drazen ambassador, leaned towards Kelly and whispered, "I think all of the local species that can tolerate breathing the air are present except for Gem, not that a cloned individual counts as a species."

"Any idea what this is all about?" Kelly whispered back, without shifting her eyes from the Vergallian home-wrecker.

"It's the first time the Verlocks have thrown a party since Drazen opened an embassy on the station," Bork replied with a shrug. "From what I've read of Earth history in that marvelous book you loaned me, that corresponds roughly to the beginning of your Bronze Age. I'd ask you what happens after all of the bronze gets used up, but I don't want to spoil the surprise."

"Libby tells me that the Verlocks were one of the founding members of the Natural League, so they've been around a long, long time. But they prefer such extreme environments that they've had relatively little to do with other species." Then Kelly stopped and blushed, realizing that she was lecturing the Drazen ambassador with facts that could hardly be news to him. "The only time I've even sat down with a Verlock before was at a meeting to settle

154

the gaming rules for the Union Station tourney that EarthCent sponsors."

"You haven't missed much," Bork told her confidentially. Then his wife asked him something and he turned away, leaving Kelly to check up on Joe and the Vergallian temptress. Her husband's voice sounded strangely stilted, and she listened carefully for a while to his story about some cavalry action he had led, before she realized that she was hearing her implant translating Joe's words from Vergallian to English. Joe had mentioned picking up languages here and there during his mercenary years, but she had never listened to him in translation before.

The Vergallian ambassador appeared to be entranced by Joe's story, and when she finally spoke, it was to invite him to dinner at her embassy. Kelly decided it was time to step in.

"How kind of you, Ambassador," she interjected, leaning forward and putting an arm awkwardly around Joe's shoulders without getting up from her chair. "We'll be happy to accept."

Whatever the Vergallian ambassador said in response was lost in another gong stroke, followed by a lot of shushing and posturing, as the gathered diplomats attempted to appear attentive before their host began to speak.

"Thank you for coming," the Verlock ambassador bellowed, while tapping his spoon on the table in rhythm with his speech. He talked at a tempo that almost approached that of a slow-spoken human, so Kelly assumed that the spoon tapping was a device to speed himself up. "Please enjoy your dinner. We will make an announcement after dessert." Then he sat down and the gong boomed a third time.

A stream of serving bots flooded the room, and they didn't even appear to be rentals. The diplomats were stunned speechless as multiple dishes of their native foods, expertly prepared, were offered up. Each species was treated to its own beverage selection, and rather than sending back one of the tall draft beers to an uncertain fate in the kitchen, Joe took all three off the tray and put one in front of Kelly. Whoever said that the way to an alien's heart was through his digestive organs must have been correct, because even the Vergallian ambassador concentrated on her own delicacies for a change.

Around the table, some of the diplomatic couples began to feed each other choice morsels, a scene Kelly could have lived without. In too short a time, the table was cleared, and a new set of serving bots appeared, bearing dessert selections and more drinks. Kelly reckoned that the cost of catering just the one meal must have been more than EarthCent's operating budget for the Union Station embassy for a decade.

But eventually, all good things come to an end. As the diplomats slumped in their places, satiated, and the table was cleared the final time, the gong sounded once more and the Verlock ambassador ponderously rose to speak.

"Throughout the ages, all intelligent beings have sought to improve their conditions and to create a better world for their offspring," the spoon-tapping Verlock began. "Unfortunately, it often happens that the hard-working, responsible species, attract the envy of those who would rather take what belongs to others than to create something new themselves. But looking around at those present tonight, I can believe the galaxy is evolving beyond such barbaric practices, thanks in no small part to our ever-reliable friends, the Stryx. Thank you for coming. Drinks will be served until the fifth gong."

The Verlock wrapped up his brief speech by sitting down in slow motion, and the noise level in the room shot up as the gathered ambassadors began to speculate excitedly. Kelly's translation implant caught scraps of conversation from around the room, like "What was that supposed to mean?" and "Did they win some galaxy-wide lottery nobody told me about?" But it was hearing the words "Why don't you come back to my place?" that got her attention.

Kelly turned and glared at the Vergallian ambassador, but she bit back her first reaction and calmly asked Joe, "What did you make of all that, Honey?"

"What?" he replied, as if his mind had been somewhere else. Then he shook the Vergallian pheromone fumes from his addled brain and turned back towards Kelly. "I, uh, I guess I wasn't listening very carefully. Something about drinks until the gong?"

"It was just a little speech about how we should all get along and not covet our neighbor's possessions," she snarled pointedly, keeping her eyes locked on the Vergallian ambassador's flawless face the whole time. The woman slowly blinked her long eyelashes, before turning away with a sigh to talk with the drunken Frunge ambassador on her other side.

"Seems like they went to a lot of work just to say something you could put on a greeting card," Joe observed. "Hey, Bork. What did you make of all that?"

The Drazen ambassador held up a finger as he listened to his wife finish saying something, then he turned to the humans. "It's unprecedented for any embassy to go to this much trouble unless they are apologizing for accidentally blowing up a world or tearing a hole in space. My wife has been having an interesting conversation with the Thark ambassador on her right, who has apparently spent the evening devouring some hand-made delicacy from Earth that they find intoxicating."

"Soap," Joe interjected, and Kelly nodded in agreement.

"The ambassador told my wife that the Tharks have been recording so many new commercial contracts for the Verlocks that they had to open an embassy on the Verlock home world. This was related in the strictest confidence, of course," he added with a wink.

Suddenly, there was a roaring sound in Kelly's ear, and she realized that the Verlock majordomo was standing right behind her. Guessing that the alien had been attempting to whisper and the volume had overwhelmed her implant, she triggered the translation to replay. Sure enough, the message was, "Our ambassador requests a private word."

"Of course," Kelly replied and stood up to follow the majordomo. On second thought, she leaned down to her husband and said, "Come on, Mr. Attaché. This is official business." As Joe rose to his feet, she flung a triumphant look at the Vergallian ambassador, and strode off behind the majordomo. Except striding after a Verlock meant moving like your feet were in a pool of molasses and you weren't in any particular hurry.

Eventually, Kelly and Joe found themselves ushered into a chamber that must have been a replica of a deep cave on the Verlock home world. The bone-white stalactites reaching down from the wet, rocky ceiling towards corresponding stalagmites on the irregular floor made the humans feel like they were walking into the mouth of an enormous rock creature with very pointy teeth. The

Verlock ambassador, whose thick skin would probably allow him to sleep on a bed of stalagmites, if that was his pleasure, waited next to a waist-high stone platform that looked like a sacrificial altar, a ceremonial dagger clenched in his three-fingered hand.

"Thank you for coming," the Verlock intoned slowly, tapping the butt of his dagger against the rock at what he no doubt believed was a break-neck tempo. "It is time we put aside our masks and spoke plainly."

"I agree," Kelly replied, not having a clue what the Verlock was talking about, but wisely choosing to get to the point as quickly as possible with the glacially slow speaker.

"You humans move too quickly," the ambassador complained. "What is this InstaNavy that has purchased three Brupt Destroyer Spheres already? Are you planning an all-out attack on the Horten systems?"

"Is this a game thing?" Kelly asked, turning to Joe.

"Yeah. They just changed the rules to allow players to pool their resources and buy serious battleships from galactic history. Blythe had the idea of buying a few and selling the shares, but she and Paul keep control. I started telling you about it last night, but you drifted off."

"Blythe? As in the BlyChas Enterprises Blythe?" the Verlock rumbled, deeply impressed.

"It's a long story," Kelly groaned, not adding that it was a long story she didn't want to get stuck telling. "You understand that they don't represent EarthCent. They are independent businessmen, uh, girls," she concluded weakly.

"Of course we know that," the Verlock responded. "Every species on the station knows that EarthCent is a remedial diplomacy school run for humans by the Stryx.

159

But BlyChas Enterprises is a business that any Verlock can admire."

"BlyChas partners with the Stryx too!" Kelly fired back in defense of EarthCent. Then she realized that she might have let the cat out of the bag and had to restrain herself from clamping her hand over her mouth. But rather than bringing the meeting to a close with a nasty comment from the ambassador about "Stryx pets," her words had the opposite effect.

"You must get me a meeting with this Blythe," the Verlock ambassador insisted. The translation implant even managed to add an overtone of pleading to his basso profondo. "It has never been our way to mix with aliens. But circumstances change, and beginning with tonight's reception, we intend to take a greater part in the galaxy's business affairs. Perhaps it is traditional with your people to accept a fee for arranging an introduction?" he hinted.

"I'll have to check with her mother first," Kelly answered with a touch of sourness. It felt like she had just been demoted from being Earth's highest ranking diplomat on the station in private conference with the powerful Verlock ambassador, to a messenger for teenage girls who still called her "Aunty." Why did the universe have to be so weird?

"We will speak again afterwards," the Verlock ambassador stated, leaving the impression that it was more of an order than an invitation. Then he ushered them slowly out of the private chamber and back to the dining hall, an exercise that reminded Joe of a childhood visit to a great-grandmother, who walked with the help of a little stand on wheels.

Kelly held onto her husband's arm as she thought through the evening's events, trying to piece together the puzzle. Joe was focused on getting back to their places in time to try another one of the excellent beers that the Verlocks must have gone to great effort to obtain. Just as they reached the table, the fifth gong sounded.

Seventeen

"I'd like the three of you to serve as my informal brain-trust," Kelly announced self-consciously. She was acutely aware that adding up the ages of Shaina, Blythe and Chastity, and then dividing by three, would yield a result of approximately half of her own age. Well, if she wanted advice from somebody older, she could always ask Joe, or Gryph for that matter. "And Blythe, I wanted to thank you for accepting the invitation to meet with the Verlock ambassador and his associates. I'm sure you'll at least get a nice meal out of it."

"I'm looking forward to it, Aunty Kelly," Blythe replied. "InstaSitter hasn't made much progress with the Verlocks because their children are practically indestructible, but I want to pitch them on the companionship angle. And besides, I figure we owed you a favor for that last commercial, so this will balance the books."

"I was a little annoyed when I saw you had used Dorothy in an advertisement without asking, even though you didn't show her face," Kelly admitted.

"Oh, not that old poster ad. This one is a fifteen-second commercial that's running on all the stations," Blythe informed her brightly. "You haven't seen it? Libby? Can you run the new spot for us?"

Before Kelly had time to digest what Blythe was saying, Libby was running the commercial on her office wall. The video started with Metoo collapsing in the grass in front of a pair of shapely, stockinged legs that sported shoes which Kelly recognized from her own closet. Then the scene changed to show Dorothy's chubby arms and small hands applying animal themed band-aids to the little robot. The voice-over declared, "If only he had an InstaSitter. Even the Stryx need looking after sometimes."

Kelly turned bright red, but she couldn't think of anything to say, especially since she had invited the girls here for help. Besides, Dorothy would probably be thrilled to see herself "taking care" of Metoo on the station's corridor display walls.

"Alright, then." Kelly took a deep breath and tried to reestablish control of the meeting's direction. "As I was saying, I hope I can count on the three of you to help me figure out what's going on around here. Shaina?" she asked, turning to the small woman with the lung capacity of a carnival barker. "Do you have anything new about changes in the local trade and the rabid interest alien businessmen are showing in Earth?"

"The wholesalers and import/export houses are in an uproar," Shaina reported. "It seems like every day brings a new surprise. I heard a weird story from one of our smugglers, I mean, importers, just this morning. She dropped off her cargo of plastic recycling at the Chintoo complex, but she couldn't pick up her usual load of sheet metal in exchange because they were out! She asked them, 'How can a robotic orbital manufacturing complex run out of sheet metal?' They answered that some other traders had placed a last-minute order, bought everything they had, and came with a small fleet of freighters to take it away. She ended up waiting a whole day in Zero-G for them to manufacture a fresh batch."

Chastity nodded. "Tinka and I have a whole sideline selling sheet metal, in the gameverse, I mean. It's kind of counter-intuitive, but setting up to smelt metal in space is a major undertaking, and making it on a planet and then transporting it into orbit costs a lot more than getting it wholesale from an orbital and paying tunnel tolls. And it's fun, because you can find a market almost anywhere you want to go."

"I don't let Paul waste our gameverse time on commodities," Blythe responded to Kelly's inquiring look. "We stick to the dangerous, high value cargoes, but neither of us really have time for trading anymore."

"Are you keeping up with your studies?" Kelly asked out of curiosity. It had been a while since Donna had mentioned anything about how the girls were progressing through the levels, and Kelly suddenly found herself wondering if they had dropped out of the Stryx education system.

"Oh, we finished that a while ago," Chastity told her. "I still have time for Raider/Trader because Mom won't let me work more at BlyChas than eight hours a day. She lets Blythe do what she wants."

"I'm almost eighteen," Blythe stated in her own defense. "Anyway, what could be a better education than working with the Stryx?"

"Thank you," Libby chipped in over the office speakers.

"So it's not that one of you has already figured out the connection between the overwhelming interest in Earth on the part of all the aliens and the changes in interstellar commerce but you're not telling me?" Kelly asked, for the sake of the record.

"No comment," Libby stated. The girls all laughed, and Blythe clapped her hands.

"How about a bet, Aunty Kelly?" Blythe suggested. "If I figure it out before you, I can use the 'Eat me up,' ad for InstaSitter that Mom wouldn't let me run."

"You're on," Kelly told her fiercely, and immediately regretted it. "You really made an ad—never mind. Of course you did." Turning her head up to speak to the ceiling, she continued, "And you, Libby. I take it that 'No comment' means the Stryx have decided it's all a matter of protected business information?"

"We've determined that all of the parties involved are acting within their own laws and are not violating any of our station, tunnel or Stryxnet usage regulations," Libby answered.

"Fine," Kelly harrumphed. She took a minute to rifle through her office junk and locate her cup of emergency instant coffee. Pulling the tab off the bottom heated the contents to barely tolerable in just five seconds. "Forgive me for not sharing, girls, but even if I had three more cups, I couldn't be that cruel. Now that I have some caffeine for back-up, can one of you explain InstaNavy to me?"

"I bought a Thark Battle Cruiser," Chastity informed her excitedly. "Everything is customizable in the gameverse so I'm making it pink. Tinka and I are going to recruit all girls for crew."

"And what is the going rate for a pink battle cruiser?" Kelly inquired, even though she was afraid to hear the answer.

"Oh, the basic model is a half million in Trader gold, but fueled up and armed to the teeth, it was close to a million."

"How did you ever find so many gamer girls to put all of that Trader gold together so quickly?" Kelly pursued the details against her better judgment.

"Oh, I paid cash, or rather, BlythChas did. We bought the Trader gold on Bill's Exchange using Stryx creds. The Stryx gave us a temporary line of credit," she added.

"What's the current exchange rate?" Shaina asked out of curiosity. She wasn't a gamer herself, but trade was trade.

"It's shot up since the rule changes," Blythe stepped in to answer. "It used to float around nine to one, but it was up to just five Trader gold for one Stryx cred this morning. All of the excess gameverse gold from trading that the players have been hoarding is getting sopped up by the military escalation."

Kelly did the math and gasped. "It's a game! How can you spend more than I've earned in my life on a single game piece?"

"We're making a profit, Aunty Kelly. Since we base our selling prices on the current exchange rate, we're actually making an eighty-percent profit just on the round-trip currency exchange. We're already way ahead on the Brupt Destroyer Spheres, and we had to buy twelve of them just to keep up with demand. Chastity didn't want to start recruiting for her ship until she finished the virtual decorating, but I bet she sells out in no time. We never could have done it without Libby to keep track of all the owners. InstaNavy has gone from nothing to over three million shareholders and enough crew for the fleet in less than a week. I think I really nailed it with the name," Blythe concluded blandly.

"Let me get this straight. You've borrowed money from the Stryx to exchange for gameverse currency, this Trader gold stuff, that you used to buy virtual battleships. Then you sold shares in the battleships for more Trader gold, which you then changed back into Stryx creds for another eighty-percent profit, and you used part of it to pay back the money you borrowed from the Stryx?" Kelly was rather proud of the way she summed it up, though she had to share the credit with the coffee.

"Yeah, it's a lot of money," Blythe replied casually. "And between InstaSitter and InstaNavy, everybody knows we're doing well, so we're getting endless invitations to invest in all sorts of alien enterprises. I assume that's why the Verlocks want to meet."

"If they're anything like the other species, watch what you say or they'll claim you've made a verbal contract when you were just being polite," Shaina warned her.

"Really? Would you come with me? It may sound like Chastity and I know what we're doing, but the truth is, we've only dealt with aliens as customers or employees to this point. The only business-to-business experience we have goes back to buying flowers, and I don't really count that because the nursery growers were human and we were just little kids," Blythe said.

"I'd love to," Shaina replied happily. "Percentage or consulting fee?"

"I think consulting makes more sense," Blythe replied. "We can work it out before the meeting. Was there anything else today, Aunty Kelly?

"Just one more thing before you go, Blythe. About our bet. If you win, you get to run the 'Eat me up,' commercial, but what do I get if I win?"

"If you win, I don't run the ad, Aunty Kelly," Blythe replied innocently.

"But you already weren't running the ad because your mother wouldn't let you," Kelly complained.

"Yeah, you really shouldn't have taken the bet," Blythe told her. Shaina and Chastity nodded in agreement, and Kelly imagined she heard Libby chiming in as well. But the chime was real, and "Collect call from Mother," appeared before her eyes.

"Accept charges," she groaned, and shrugged at the girls. Chastity and Blythe understood immediately what was up, and Chastity explained it to Shaina, who had never heard of anybody calling collect. Shaina gave Kelly a sympathetic wave, and the three girls left the ambassador alone in her office.

"Kelly, I'm just a week away now. I can't tell you how wonderfully everybody treats me when they find out that you're my daughter. I suspect the ship steward has been spreading it around, because I have nonstop invitations from the sweetest aliens to discuss business opportunities. The aliens are so cute, and their start-ups are so much more interesting than all the gaming businesses on Earth."

"Did you buy that real estate on Thuri Minor?" Kelly asked.

"I went with a variable option pegged to the Stryx cred, so I have three months to decide whether to close at the current price or forfeit a modest option fee. But since when were you interested in financial affairs, Kelly?"

"Hey, I keep up with the Trader gold exchange rates and stuff like that," Kelly bluffed. "So why did you decide to hold off?"

"Well, I gave it some thought, and it occurred to me I should wait to take a look at the real estate on Union Station." A long pause ensued while Kelly's mother waited for her reaction.

"That's great, Mom," Kelly said cautiously, after she recovered enough to speak. "It's really expensive, though.

The human population just keeps on growing because it's the ideal place to do business."

"That's what makes a good investment, Kelly. Do you think I want to buy cheap real estate in a place that everybody is leaving? I could do that on Earth!"

"Oh, right," Kelly admitted with grudging admiration.

"Anyway, I just wanted to tell you that everything is on schedule and I'll be showing up at your door in time for dinner next Friday. See you then," she rang off, without even waiting for Kelly's acknowledgement.

"Does everybody in the galaxy understand more about business than I do?" Kelly asked plaintively, looking up at the ceiling.

"Was that a question for me?" Libby replied immediately.

"No, I was just talking to myself," Kelly replied, sounding a bit deflated.

"I'm always here if you need to speak to somebody," Libby reminded her gently. "And the galaxy is a very big place. I'm sure there are plenty of people who don't understand business any better than you do."

Kelly parsed the sentence looking for something positive and gave up with a sigh.

"Don't forget that you are one of the top diplomats in EarthCent service, and between you and me, you're our favorite," Libby added. "But I can't understand why you drink such awful coffee that's fortified with depressants. It's really intended for human workers in high oxygen environments who get a little too euphoric. I wasn't going to say anything before, but you don't even have a prescription for it, do you?"

Prescription coffee with depressants? That would teach her to buy white-labeled food products in the Shuk without bringing Shaina along.

Eighteen

Joe and Kelly stood uncomfortably in the airlock of the Horten embassy, waiting for the decontamination process to complete. Kelly had procrastinated accepting the Horten invitation for as long as was diplomatically possible, because Donna had told her about their pathological fear of biological contamination. At some point in their history, the Hortens had fought a war with microbes, and the aftermath had traumatized them so severely that the whole civilization was obsessed with cleanliness.

"Is my radiation badge changing colors?" Kelly asked Joe nervously, pointing to the band of treated plastic around her wrist that had been supplied by the decontamination attendant.

"I would say that you're medium-well done," Joe jested, after making a show of studying the bracelet. When Kelly failed to laugh, he recanted. "It's not a radiation badge, it's a sort of a mood bracelet. I thought you were too nervous to understand what that Horten attendant was saying, and she did speak awfully fast."

"A mood bracelet? Like from when we were little?"

"When you were little, maybe," Joe tried to sound offended. "Real men don't wear mood bracelets."

"I admit it, I wasn't listening. So is this the Horten idea of a party favor, like they're trying to make us feel at home?" Kelly asked.

"It's actually a very smart idea," Joe explained. "She didn't go into detail about the technology, but it's supposed to enhance communications between species by translating the mood of the wearer into colors. Translation implants don't always do a great job reproducing the emotional tone of the words, and it would take a better poker player than me to read anything from alien faces. You have to grow up around them for that kind of understanding."

"Mine seems to have turned pale yellow, while yours is more bluish. What did they say it means?"

"She didn't explain the color codes," Joe admitted. "Besides, it doesn't matter, since I doubt the Hortens will be wearing bracelets. If I had to guess, I'd say that pale yellow means nervous and bluish means thirsty."

A red light flashed over the door and there was a loud wail from a siren. Kelly grabbed Joe's arm, wondering if they failed the decontamination process and were about to get flushed, and she prepared to call Libby for a rescue. But the light and the siren just meant the decontamination process was complete, and the door leading into the embassy reception room slid open. A slender Horten wearing the top hat of authority strode forward to greet them.

"I am Ambassador Ortha," he said, stopping about two feet away. There was something odd about the sound of his voice, so Joe flipped the mental switch to turn off his implant and listened for the next sentence.

"I am Ambassador Kelly McAllister, and this is my husband, Joe," Kelly replied. "Thank you for inviting us to your embassy."

"We have done you a great honor," the ambassador replied immodestly, and Joe instantly realized that his voice was coming from a speaker, rather than from the Horten's mouth. That could only mean one thing, so he put out his arm to stop Kelly as she took an uncertain step forward.

"Glass wall," he told her. "Apparently, we failed decontamination after all."

"It is unfortunate," the Horten ambassador confirmed Joe's guess. "I would have grudgingly risked your physical presence and later undergone decontamination myself, but my family and several prominent members of our community are in attendance. I imagine you understand."

Kelly squinted at the ambassador, and then tried looking across the hall at an angle, but she couldn't see any indication of a glass wall. With the Horten just standing there as if he was waiting for them to do something, she cautiously extended her arm until her fingers made contact with an impossibly smooth, cool surface. She jerked her hand away, leaving a set of prints.

"I see we were correct to be cautious," the ambassador stated, sounding rather satisfied. "The decontamination technician said something about not wanting to draw all of the oils from your skin, but warned that they could be solvents for our own vital fluids. A long shot, I grant you, but why take chances? Dinner will be served in the isolation booth." Having satisfied himself with his explanations, he made a gesture, and the transparent walls began to glow with a soft orange light.

"Looks like a hallway leading to an isolation booth," Joe commented, tapping the wine bottle against his hip, where it clinked reassuringly off of his antique Swiss army knife. It looked like he might be in need of the rarely used corkscrew attachment tonight. He exchanged shrugs with Kelly, and they walked down the glass tube, arriving in what appeared to be a well-appointed dining hall. But the orange glow showed that two of the place settings were actually isolated in a glass box that cut right through the table, extending from the floor to some point above their heads.

"Well, this is cozy," Kelly murmured, feeling like an exhibition at the zoo. The pale yellow of her mood bracelet had acquired a darker tint, while Joe's bluish band remained unchanged. As soon as they took their seats, the Hortens entered the room from two different doorways and filled up the rest of the places. With the exception of the ambassador, they all wore a filmy plastic sleeve over their evening wear, as if they had come from the dry cleaners and forgotten to remove the protective bags.

"Before dinner is served, I'd like to propose a toast to our human guests," the ambassador announced, standing directly across the table from the isolation booth. The Hortens passed around bottles of a green liquid and filled their own glasses, while Joe quickly plied the Swiss army knife to open the traditional bottle of gift wine. He barely got the cork out and filled their glasses in time for the ambassador's toast. "May our past misunderstandings become the basis for our future relations."

"What does that mean?" Joe asked Kelly, after they each took a sip of their wine. It proved to be an excellent choice, and Joe was relieved they weren't wasting it on their hosts.

"I think it's something like forgive and forget, but in reverse," she whispered back. "Do you think they're waiting for me to make a toast in reply?" Without waiting for an answer, she raised her glass again, cleared her throat and toasted, "And may our future relations begin this night."

Joe thought it was a clever formulation that dovetailed nicely into the Horten ambassador's ambiguous toast, but the Hortens made no reaction at all, and none of them even bothered raising their own glasses. Indeed, they were all engaged in making food choices from a holographic carousel that had started making the rounds of the large oval table like a model train. Each Horten it passed chose a holographic entrée and several side dishes by removing them from the carousel, an impressive trick of technology that was new to the humans.

The ethereal representations of the menu items winked and shimmered before each guest, serving as orders for the waiters, who began making the rounds with the real food. Although some of the items were aesthetically pleasing, Horten foodstuffs were generally regarded as poisonous to humans, and neither Joe nor Kelly was inclined to test that thesis.

All during the period that the Hortens were being served, Kelly sat patiently. She assumed that they would soon be receiving a consignment of take-out food from a human restaurant, the way the different species usually dealt with the dietary requirements of alien guests. But when the Hortens all began eating, she started getting annoyed.

"Excuse me," she said loudly, trying to maintain a look of dignity. "The invitation didn't say anything about supplying our own food!"

None of the Hortens even glanced in their direction.

"I don't think the isolation chamber is wired for two-way sound," Joe told her with a sudden grin. "Either that or it's not turned on. Let me give it a try." With that, he leaned forward and rapped the glass sharply with his knuckles. The resulting sounds were more like dull clunks than knocks, reminding him of the armored glass on a fighting vehicle. But it was enough to catch the attention of the Hortens, who jabbed each other and pointed at the humans.

"Is something wrong?" the Horten ambassador inquired, his voice coming from above and slightly behind them.

"We didn't bring our own dinner!" Kelly replied in frustration, and pantomimed eating soup with a spoon in case the ambassador still couldn't hear. The Horten turned a shade of light red and turned to say something to the chief server, who immediately turned a bright yellow.

Joe nudged Kelly and said, "I guess that explains the mood bracelets. They're just trying to level the field."

"My apologies," Ambassador Ortha said. "The isolation booth has not been used since the embassy was remodeled a few cycles ago. Apparently the voice circuits from your side aren't operational, and the one-way glass is also malfunctioning."

"Libby?" Kelly subvoced, not wanting to look like an imbecile who continued talking after being told that nobody could hear her. "Have you been watching all of this? Can you patch me through over whatever they have for an audio system on the other side?"

"If you wish," Libby replied with a hint of amusement in her voice. "Starting now."

"I've requested technical help from the Stryx," Kelly said, watching for the Horten reaction. None of the guests jerked their heads up in surprise at the sound of her voice, but the pale blue skin that most of the Hortens had been sporting just a moment or two earlier turned a molted

176

shade of green, with some showing additional streaks of grey. Kelly looked over at Joe and mouthed, "Oops."

The Horten ambassador either had better control over his emotions, or a different agenda than his family and fellows, because he only turned a little redder. "I see you don't mince words. Your message has been received loud and clear, so let me be equally plain," he declared in a steely voice. "The servers were reluctant to deliver the special food we ordered and decontaminated for you because they were afraid that my other guests would be sickened if they chanced to look in your direction. But there's no need to call upon your Stryx allies in a panic. If you just wait patiently for a minute, we'll handle this situation ourselves!"

Joe leaned in until his lips were practically touching Kelly's ear, and whispered, "Green for envy, grey for depression, and red for anger?"

Surveying the now colorful display of Hortens at the dinner table, Kelly nodded in agreement. Then it occurred to her to look at Joe's bracelet, which had gone from slightly bluish back to the original white after he drank a glass of wine. Her own mood had shifted from a nervous yellow to a light red, and that was fading away even as she watched.

"It's not so hard to understand why they act the way they do," she whispered back to Joe. As much as she hated to admit it, she was beginning to feel a little sorry for the Hortens and their overstated emotions. "Now that I think of it, all of the times I've seen Hortens in public, they've been wearing some kind of environmental suit so you couldn't see their skin. I thought it was to shield them from contamination, but maybe it's just to protect their privacy."

"I wish I could get some of these guys in a poker game," Joe responded with a marked lack of empathy.

Suddenly, two Horten serving men appeared with rags and buckets and began washing the glass of the isolation booth. For some reason, whatever soap they were using clung thickly to the glass, rendering it an opaque swirly white. In less than a minute, the humans were truly in isolation, unable to see more than suggestions of shadowy movements on the other side of the glass.

"You see that we have our own methods of coping without turning to the Stryx for every little thing," the now invisible Horten ambassador stated dryly. "I apologize for the delay, of course, but your dinner will be served momentarily."

True to the ambassador's word, a cylindrical glass tube descended from the ceiling of the booth. The bottom of the cylinder contained a variety of plated entrees, which looked like they had been unceremoniously dumped out of take-out containers onto glass plates. Still, the Chinese food smelled delicious, and Joe promptly claimed the franks-and-beans. After they each withdrew what they intended to eat, the cylinder rose back into the ceiling.

Unable to see what the rest of the company was doing and receiving no further word from the ambassador, Kelly and Joe began to eat. The meal passed in a sort of uncomfortable silence, so perhaps the Hortens had disabled their audio feed, or maybe it was customary for the aliens to eat without conversation. Having no desire to prolong the evening, both of the humans ate quickly.

Kelly finished first for a change and pushed away her plate, in case the serving staff was watching from above for clues. Joe wiped up the last of the beans with a heel of pumpernickel a minute later and followed suit. Almost immediately, the soapy whitewash began disappearing from the walls of the isolation booth in broad swathes, revealing the same Horten serving men, this time wielding squirt bottles and rubber squeegees. Whatever their quirks, the Hortens sure knew how to clean glass. They also knew how to make themselves scarce, because other than the serving men, the only Hortens remaining were the ambassador and a few other hat wearers.

"Thank you for respecting our customs," the ambassador said with what sounded like a tinge of sarcasm, but Kelly could never be sure with the implant technology. The angry red tint had vanished from Ortha's skin, and he now showed a neutral beige. The other Hortens were similarly colored, though perhaps with a hint of yellow that made them look like old ivory.

"Misunderstandings are the rule when members of different species sit together for the first time," Kelly replied, placing a slight stress on "together." Let's see what your translator makes of that, she thought with satisfaction.

"I don't want to spar with you, so let's get down to business," Ortha replied. "The Earth fleet, managed by humans under your direct control, is planning an attack on Horten space. Our intelligence reports confirm that the admiral is the adopted son of your military attaché, and the owners of InstaNavy are the daughters of the EarthCent embassy office manager. Do you dare deny it?"

Kelly immediately felt her eyelids begin to droop and she kicked herself for drinking that last glass of wine. Then she recalled her duty and pulled herself together enough to ask, "What's to deny? You're talking about the gameverse. EarthCent has no policy about gameverse activities whatsoever. And in my case, EarthCent has no interest in gameverse activities!"

Kelly's bracelet turned a darkish red, perhaps expressing sleepy anger, while the Horten ambassador turned a brighter shade of the same color. The other Hortens slipped farther into the yellow palette.

"Do you really mean to claim that EarthCent isn't working towards establishing itself as the primary gameverse superpower?" the ambassador thundered at her.

"Gameverse superpower?" Kelly shot back in disgust. "What's that green stuff you guys are drinking out there? Why should anybody possibly care what happens in the gameverse?"

"You tell 'em, Ambassador," Joe egged her on. Although supporting Raider/Trader had become his main business, there was something about the over-the-top seriousness with which everybody was treating the game that put his teeth on edge. Besides, it was fun watching Kelly get mad at somebody else for a change.

The remaining Hortens all stood up and gathered in a little clump, not unlike a huddle. Joe poured a final glass of wine for his wife and himself to finish the bottle, and they sipped in silence while the Hortens attempted to come up with an answer to Kelly's question. Finally, the huddle broke up, and the ambassador addressed Kelly again.

"Either you're playing some kind of deep game or you are truly ignorant of diplomacy," Ortha stated flatly. "From our intelligence reports of your meetings with other species, you are capable of either."

"So why don't you explain to me what's so important about who shoots who in the gameverse, and then we'll all be on the same page," Kelly retorted.

"Surely you understand that the Stryx will not allow any of the species using their tunnel network to openly engage in interstellar war with each other," the ambassador explained. "So what could war in the gameverse be other than a proxy for the real thing?"

"That's the dumbest thing I've heard in my twenty years of service," Kelly exploded. "Were you planning on handing over your home world to a bunch of gamers if they win? Are you all taking bets on the outcome? Is anybody's job at stake?"

The skin color of the Hortens shaded towards purple, and Joe muttered, "Embarrassment?"

"Apparently we misunderstood your intentions," the ambassador mumbled, and cast a significant look at Kelly's Horten-supplied bracelet. "Either that, or you are capable of deceiving our lie-detecting device, which my technicians assure me is not possible."

"Apology accepted," Kelly stated archly. "I will take it on faith that you didn't mean to deceive us either."

"Deceive you?" Ortha began making loud snapping noises, and the other Hortens joined in as well, their skin turning a cheerful brown. It took Kelly a while to figure out that they were laughing uncontrollably. "Hortens do not lie, Madam Ambassador. Even the slightest falsehood causes our skin to break out in a terrible rash. The chemical agent that permanently altered our genome this way nearly put an end to our species. Everybody seems to think we introduced biological weapons in a terrible civil war, but in fact, the opposite was true. It was a badly engineered cosmetic product that changed us into what we are, and the civil war was merely the logical outcome of our people losing the ability to lie to one another."

"Well, then. I think we've taken a major step forward tonight in interspecies understanding," Kelly ventured. "Why don't we plan on meeting again at a future date and finding out what we really have in common?"

181

"Are you sure you don't want to continue tonight?" the ambassador inquired. "There are many details about the new game rules we would like to discuss with you."

"Oh, I'd love to stay," Kelly replied. "But we really need to be getting home. My daughter wasn't feeling well and the sitter is expecting us at any minute."

The Hortens all broke out in snapping laughter again, this time pointing at Kelly and slapping each other's fingers down. Joe leaned over and said, "Uh, Kel? Check your bracelet."

It turned out that black was the color of lies. To the vast amusement of the Hortens, Kelly's face turned fire engine red.

Nineteen

When the much-anticipated confrontation between battle fleets led by the humans and the Hortens did take place, it was a fiasco. Both sides had chosen to invest heavily in Brupt Destroyer Spheres due to their unequaled fire-power, so they all found themselves in the same literal boat. Their gameverse leaders had felt compelled to order the unprepared capital ships into battle, just in case the other side brought theirs.

That both sides had expected the outcome did little to assuage the egos of the men crewing the titanic virtual ships. But the crews hadn't had enough time to figure out what their vessels were capable of, much less how to operate the holographic controls that had been designed for the Brupt. It didn't help matters that the Brupt had relied on group telepathy rather than comms for coordinating crew actions and for inter-ship communications. All Paul could do was to watch the disaster unfold on the main viewer.

The sole bright spot for either side was the pink Thark Battle Cruiser, co-captained by Chastity and Tinka, and remotely crewed by thirty-two-hundred adolescent gamer girls from a dozen different species. It turned out that the Thark ship ran on a massively redundant control-by-consensus system, reflecting the highly egalitarian Thark warrior society of a distant past. In order to counteract the suicidal heroics and self-sacrificing tendencies of Thark officers, the control system was designed so that every crewmember could issue navigational and fire control commands, but the ship would only respond when the consensus agreed with the instructions of one of the co-captains.

The Pink Death, as the ship quickly became known, moved jerkily through the gameverse battlespace, firing only on occasion, and accidentally running down many of the original two-player vessels that had accompanied the big ships. Since the girls had reached an early consensus that defensive shields and countermeasures were excellent ideas, none of the weapons carried by the small ships could harm them. With the crews of Brupt ships on both sides unable to coordinate the firing of their weapons with target acquisition and command, the Pink Death would have carried the day for Earth, except for a small flaw in the recruitment process.

It turned out that many of the girls who had bought into Chastity's ship, and who were crewing over Stryxnet from the comfort of their bedroom mock-ups, lived on Horten and its allied worlds. It hadn't occurred to anybody to establish a loyalty test for crew membership, since the men self-segregated without being told. But girls from all over the galaxy, most of whom were between the ages of twelve and sixteen and weren't allowed to buy into the male-officered ships, only had the one option.

After much futile maneuvering around Brupt Destroyer Spheres to attain advantageous firing positions, only to have their weapons systems report a consensus failure lockout, Chastity and Tinka decided that their time would be better spent practicing navigation with thousands of hands on the controls. So they declared victory, and easily reached a consensus to go off and play by themselves.

On the bridge of the lead Brupt Destroyer Sphere in the Earth fleet, Blythe watched the Pink Death sail away from the battlespace and sighed. She had never been a huge fan of fighting herself, but it was a necessary part of the Raider/Trader game. The holographic projection of the Brupt bridge made her wonder if the long-since-exiled aliens knew of any colors other than black and red. Why Paul had refused to follow Chastity's lead and redecorate was beyond her.

"Joe certainly got this one right," Paul commented to Dring, who had come along for the ride. "He said that even if the controls were simple, it would take us months of real-time practice to learn how to fight with a ship this big, and years to really understand its capabilities in combat."

"Why didn't you ask the Stryx for help?" Dring inquired.

"He wouldn't," Blythe answered for Paul. "I did, but Gryph said the game was too closely coupled with real-universe economics for them to show favoritism. Not that the Stryx get everything right. Jeeves predicted that neither side would have enough control over the Brupt ships to actually fight them, but he also thought that the girls would destroy all of us just to make a point."

A holographic projection of a panting ensign appeared on the bridge. The poor kid had probably been running little circles for five minutes in his own mock-up, as a virtual reality of corridors, hatches and ramps rolled by around him.

"Ensign Hart reporting from main engineering, Admiral. The chief engineer has made no progress on rerouting fire control to the bridge or integrating target acquisition systems with fire control. He says, no offense, Sir, that even if we removed you from the loop, there's still a seven-minute delay getting a runner from the targeting section to the firing controls. By the time we fire, the target will have moved. The ship just wasn't designed for non-telepaths."

"Tell him to keep trying, Ensign," Paul answered. "We have another three hours in the gameverse so we may as well use them."

"The chief did say something about bringing homing pigeons next time, Admiral."

"You and the pigeons are dismissed, Ensign," Paul barked, trying to hide his amusement under the gruffness of authority. At least his crew members were thinking creatively, but obviously, homing pigeons wouldn't work in the gameverse. The only practical solution was to upgrade the virtual Destroyer Spheres with modern comms, but the game programmers weren't selling them yet. If they had put all of the money into Thark Battle Cruisers, they would have dominated the battlespace, even with the annoying consensus controls.

"So, do you believe this is the outcome the game pro-grammers expected when they changed the rules?" Dring followed up on his earlier question.

"That's it, Dring!" Blythe exclaimed. She swiveled her chair around to face the friendly alien, since nothing of interest was happening on the main viewer anyway. The only real fighting was between the clouds of little pickets, which as in previous battles, were evenly matched. "We thought we were playing a game, but in reality, the game is playing with us! But what do the programmers have to gain by antagonizing the player base?"

186

"There's tens of millions in Trader gold sunk into these ships, and a lot of it was purchased on the exchange with real currency," Paul added. "The way BlyChas structured the shares, most of our owners don't have much at risk. But the guys who bought commissions won't be too happy if they turn out to be officering ghost ships."

"We spread the ownership shares much thinner than necessary in order to keep the cost per-player low, just in case something like this happened," Blythe explained to Dring. "And Paul, if it makes sense to buy new ships, we can always transfer the commissions. It would have minimal impact on our profits. Scrapping the fleet and starting over would actually be a great business proposition for us, but I still want to know why they tricked us into buying ships we couldn't make use of in the first place."

"Maybe they're just testing your commitment," Dring suggested. "While they have a tremendous amount of data about how players conduct themselves in the game, they don't have any way of knowing whether the whole thing is just a fad. The galaxy-wide adoption of a multi-player game using the Stryxnet for infrastructure is something nobody has seen before."

"I know a bit about the history of human gaming from my dad," Blythe ventured. "The massive multiplayer games usually build up users quickly, peak, and then go into decline, unless there are new releases that expand the gameverse. Dad had never heard of a major game that basically used the current state of the real universe as a model for the gameverse before Raider/Trader, much less one that forces players to spend most of their time in the game simply traveling from place to place to earn game currency by trading. He says that most of the players don't fit the usual gamer profile. A lot of the kids actually see it as a way to look around the galaxy and learn something about business. And then the huge demand for Trader gold means that the good players can make a sort of a living at it."

"Perhaps the game programmers are feeling their way, just like the players," Dring suggested to Blythe, sounding rather amused by his own analysis.

"Well, according to the InstaNavy shareholder records, the players are much younger than I would have guessed. That may be why they accepted Paul as a leader so easily. At eighteen, he's right around the average age. In fact..."

"Uh-oh," Paul interrupted Blythe. "You might have been a bit hasty, what you said about Jeeves being wrong earlier."

Chastity and Tinka were back, and the girls had come to a consensus after all. They were shooting at everything, especially the Destroyer Spheres, which exploded with brilliant displays as the Thark weapons destabilized their fusion cores. The previous jerky movements and random weapons discharges from the Pink Death had been re-placed by silky smooth turns and concentrated displays of lethality.

The destruction of both fleets was sped along by the fact that the weapons crews on the Destroyer Spheres broke discipline and started firing blindly, in an attempt to get their money's worth out of the ordnance before the girls rendered it moot.

"Want to ask her to spare us for old time's sake?" Paul suggested to Blythe.

"How? Write a giant message in space? I'd rather get home early," Blythe replied philosophically. "Besides, it makes good business sense. She's saved us from having to convince our shareholders to abandon these ships and buy something new. It's really pretty smart of her, now that I think about it."

"Too late now anyway," Paul reported with a groan. "Our own crew is firing everything we've got, and if I'm reading this tactical display correctly, the Brupt ship that I thought Patches was running just launched most of their torpedoes in our direction."

"If the game programmers anticipated all of this with their rule changes, then they're better at forecasting outcomes than I am," Dring admitted. "So what happens now?"

Paul made a half-hearted attempt to maneuver the giant spherical ship out of the path of the rapidly closing torpedoes, but there was no escape. The gameverse suddenly disappeared around them, leaving them sitting in a small mock-up with the ship's controller flashing the message, "Game Over."

Twenty

Kelly went by herself to meet her mother at the passenger liner dock and escort her back to Mac's Bones. Kelly's mother talked about trivialities on the tube ride home, and despite all of her personal and professional progress in the years since they had last met, Kelly still felt like she had been caught trying to get away with something. Joe and Dorothy were waiting to meet them when they arrived.

"Please call me Marge," Kelly's mother's hastened to say to Joe before Kelly could introduce them. This immediately threw Kelly off balance, since last she knew her mother's name was Deborah, but she let it slide rather than starting things off on the wrong foot.

"Joe McAllister, Marge." Joe and Kelly's mother shook hands, and then exchanged hugs. "I'm honored to meet you at last. I've been waiting five years to thank you for bringing up such a fine daughter."

"What a coincidence," Kelly's mother exclaimed. "I've been waiting five years to thank you for taking her off my hands. And now I can thank you for this scrumptious granddaughter as well." Having established their common interest in Kelly and Dorothy as joint property, Joe and Marge each took one of Dorothy's hands and strolled towards the picnic tables set up outside the ice harvester for the occasion.

Hoping to soften the blow of her mother's descent on paradise, Kelly had opted to invite Donna's family and a few others to the welcoming meal. In a master stroke of strategic planning, Kelly convinced Jeeves to attend and to sit next to her mother, who insisted on having Dorothy on her other side, with Joe next to Dorothy.

Kelly sat next to Donna and Stan across the table, along with Metoo, who liked to sit where he could see Dorothy. Donna's girls, along with Tinka, Paul and Patches, took up the rest of the table, leaving a spot for Laurel at the end. Laurel had insisted on doing the cooking, which meant she was up and down through the first half of the meal. Dring had been invited, but he claimed a prior commitment.

All of Kelly's fears of embarrassing stories about her childhood being recounted by her tone-deaf mother went for naught. Marge's attention through the first part of the meal was captivated by Dorothy's imaginative account of how she and Metoo had spent the day "esploring." Kelly could tell from Joe's occasional quizzical glances in her direction that she might have oversold the thesis that her mother was a ticking time bomb of anti-social behavior waiting to go off at the slightest provocation.

As they finished eating, Dorothy got around to asking her grandmother the natural question about who her mommy was, which gave Marge a reason to run through the news about the rest of the family on Earth.

"Your Aunt Lisa has been married for ages, and she has three little boys, only they aren't so little anymore. In fact, the oldest one is just as tall as that handsome young man sitting at the end of the table," Marge told Dorothy.

"Paul!" Dorothy identified him proudly.

191

"And your Uncle Peter has two girls with a boy in between. The younger girl is just about your age, and her name is Susan."

"I like Susan," Dorothy announced. "I want her to come and visit me."

"Your grandpa Steve, my husband, is on a fishing vacation with Susan's other grandpa, Harold. Do you have any fish on Union Station?"

Dorothy looked uncertain, but across the table, Metoo raised a pincer excitedly, as if he was back in kindergarten on a Parents Day.

"Yes, Metoo?" Kelly's mother asked observantly.

"We have lots of fish from all over the galaxy," the little Stryx reported. "Some of them are very nice people."

"Thank you, Metoo," Marge continued politely. "Grandpa Steve should be finishing his fishing trip tomorrow, and then he's going to go stay with Grandpa Harold in Buffalo until I get home."

"Bubbalo!" Dorothy exclaimed, thrilled to have the opportunity to use such a difficult word again.

"Bubbalo?" Kelly interrupted her conversation with Donna about the spots on predatory felines to stare across the table at her mother.

"Buffalo," her mother corrected Kelly, and turned back to Dorothy. "Pronunciation is very important. When your mother was a little girl, she used to raise her hand in school and say she had to go to the bat room, so all the other children made fun of her."

"Who is in Buffalo?" Kelly asked, barely noticing her mother's first embarrassing story of the evening.

"Your brother's in-laws are from Buffalo," her mother told her. "You'd know that if you ever came to visit.

They're very nice people, though they do tend to go on about the Bills."

"Oh. They're having trouble getting by?" Kelly inquired sympathetically.

"Not that kind of bills, silly," her mother retorted. "The Buffalo Bills. The professional football team. There aren't enough people left living in the area to even fill the stadium, so they have to play half of their games in Toronto, but all of the locals who haven't left the planet are big fans."

"Isn't Buffalo the place that used to get buried in snow ten times a winter?" Joe asked, just to show he was paying attention. "I seem to remember that from the news when I was a kid. I always wished I could live there so I could get days off from school."

"Why would anybody keep living in a place like that now?" asked the ever-practical Donna. "What kind of work can anyone get in a city that can't fill its own stadium?"

"Funny you should ask that," Marge replied. "Just last year, Harold was getting so depressed from watching the city decay around him that he talked about abandoning the house to rot and moving to be closer to the grandchildren. But then, one of those new start-up businesses that come out of nowhere took off, and all of a sudden, people are moving to Buffalo in droves to work there."

"What business is that?" Kelly asked quietly, as she dipped her dinner knife in the spaghetti sauce left on her plate and doodled something.

"I think it's called Bill's Change or something like that," her mother replied casually. "They have something to do with games or money, I don't remember the details."

"Bill's Exchange, in Buffalo, with all the Stryx cred commission money from selling Trader gold," Blythe

193

yelled from the end of the table. "I win. We get to run the commercial."

"Ha!" Kelly shot back holding up her plate. "What does that say, smarty pants?"

"You think my spaghetti sauce was too runny?" Laurel asked. She sounded a bit hurt as she broke off her conversation with Patches, who was about to explain the origin of his nickname.

"No, not you, Laurel," Kelly replied in exasperation, jerking the plate down. Sure enough, her hastily improvised lettering had slumped and elongated, but she thought she could still make out the scrawl. "Here, Donna. You read this," she said, pushing the plate in front of her friend.

"Buff attack - share goldmine?" Donna deciphered the droopy hieroglyphics.

"Exactly!" Kelly pronounced triumphantly. "The attack on Buffalo the Stryx foiled a few months ago was the game makers sending a message to the moneychangers to share the profits, or else. I win, so you can't run the 'Eat me up!' commercial."

"Somebody attacked Buffalo?" Marge demanded. "Does anybody care to explain to me what you are all talking about?" She turned to Jeeves, who had been quietly observing or talking softly with Paul through most of the meal. "How about you, Mr. Jeeves? Everybody I've met during the trip says you can always trust the Stryx."

"Certainly, Mrs. Frank," Jeeves responded politely. "There was an incident a few months ago in which a large asteroid was detected on an interception course with Earth. We sent a science vessel to do some careful measurements and projected the impact point to be Buffalo. Nobody was ever in real danger, so it's likely that your

194

daughter was correct in describing it as part of a business negotiation."

"I remember that from the news," Marge replied, her voice rising. "They said that if the asteroid hadn't been detected, it could have caused a global extinction event. That was part of a business negotiation?"

"Of course, we were aware of all the Stryx creds flowing into Earth, but we try not to pry into private business affairs," Jeeves continued calmly. "The currency flow was distributed amongst locations all over the world, so the footprint of Bill's Exchange in Buffalo was actually quite small in the scale of things. They probably spread the money around the globe to avoid the attention of your remaining tax authorities."

"But why did I get all of the dinner invitations?" Kelly pressed Jeeves. "I know the Stryx don't want to show favoritism with competitive information, but now we've figured out where the money was coming from and why it was going to Earth. Libby showed us the Stryx cred flow months ago, but large as that was, Earth's economy is still small beans compared with any of the older species. Why did they all descend on Earth like locusts?"

"Gryph and the others aren't happy about this, but I'm going to tell you anyway. And the reason I'm going to tell you is that it won't change anything," Jeeves said, almost sadly. "Do you remember being asked to the Grenouthian embassy, before all the other invitations started coming in?"

"Of course," Kelly answered. "Joe had a terrible allergic reaction to the bunny fur."

"The Grenouthians run their own entertainment network, and they produce quite a few documentaries about other species, which their population seems to find quite

195

amusing. All of the interest in Earth began with a documentary about your pre-Stryx economic system."

"Hard to believe the older species had something to learn from our market economies," Stan interjected. "I spent a few years working on a doctoral dissertation, applying game theory to economic history, before I decided the system was all rigged in the old days. I dropped out to work in real gaming."

"Why didn't you ever mention that before, Stanley?" Donna asked in wonder.

"I was ashamed it took me so long to figure out," he confessed.

"Unfortunately, your assumption that the Grenouthians weren't interested in Earth for the sake of your knowledge is correct," Jeeves picked up where he had left off. "The main focus of the documentary, which ended up breaking viewership records and getting translated into most of the popular languages in the galaxy, was the human affinity for Ponzi schemes."

"Oh, you're pulling our legs," Kelly's mother said, and gave Jeeves a playful push.

"Given the opportunity, most humans will choose to entrust their savings to whoever promises them the highest rate of return," Jeeves explained. "The human implementation of financial markets which were utterly detached from the supposed underlying assets was unique in the galaxy. If it wasn't for Bill's Exchange, the other species would have gotten a good laugh from the documentary, and that would have been the end of it. But the combination of your financial gullibility with a significant inflow of Stryx creds proved too attractive for any entrepreneurial species to ignore."

"I did quite a bit of research about historical real estate prices, and excluding a few boom towns, I came to the conclusion that prices were strictly a function of interest rates and how much money the government was printing," Stanley chipped in.

"Correct," Jeeves said approvingly. "The value of your assets was defined by the supply of money, which was arbitrarily controlled by your governmental banking authorities. It's the exact opposite of how the rest of the galaxy does things. Of course, barter is always preferred, but where currency is necessary, it should be valued based on the backing assets, not the other way around. And that brings us to why the Stryx opened Earth when we did."

"I heard it was because the Vergallians were getting ready to move in and add us to their empire, whether we wanted to or not," Joe ventured.

"No, the Stryx only step in and interfere with the natural developments of a species and their place in the galaxy if we judge they are in imminent danger of unintentionally destroying themselves," Jeeves said seriously. "You were actually progressing quite quickly for a species so far from the galactic center, and given a few hundred years, you would have developed a crude interstellar capability by your own efforts, probably using ships carrying frozen embryos with robot tenders."

"How could you just assume we were going to destroy ourselves?" Kelly protested. "I've studied a lot of Earth history, and the relations between the biggest nations were pretty good when the Stryx came. In fact, I've read that even if one nation could have destroyed another without retaliation, they probably wouldn't have, because of their economic ties."

197

"My elders weren't worried about Earth's national rivalries," Jeeves explained patiently. "The imminent danger was a global economic collapse, brought on by your bizarre financial system and your global addiction to pyramid schemes. Wars sparked by economic collapse are the worst kind. They push civilizations back into their stone age, or to total extinction."

"Sounds like humans were real losers," Chastity commented from the end of the table.

"If any of you are looking for a great investment, I have a tunnel on Drazen I could sell you," Tinka added, and the two girls dissolved into laughter.

"What about all this business with the reorganization of mercenary forces and the new trade routes we went to scope out?" Joe asked the Stryx, still smarting from the loss of a keg tap.

"Probably the Verlocks," Kelly answered with a burst of insight. "If not the Verlocks, whoever created this annoying game that all of the kids are playing. They're mining the data from the trades in the gameverse, like Blythe suggested, and they're using it to make a killing in the real universe."

"I think I'd like to invest with these Verlocks," Kelly's mother mused. "It sounds like a sure thing."

"I've been meeting the local Verlocks about business. Do you want me to ask for you?" Blythe offered helpfully. "How much are you looking to invest?"

Kelly sat back with a smug little grin, ready to enjoy seeing her mother embarrassed for the first time, ever.

"I think about a million Stryx cred would be a good start," Marge replied. "I took a hit on corn contracts when it rained right through the Midwest harvest season this year, so I'm a little cash poor."

The blood all drained from Kelly's face as she stared across the table. "What are you talking about, Mother. You never even made enough money in your bake shop to pay for the electricity!"

"That's why I got interested in commodities trading," her mother replied. "I wanted to hedge the cost of sugar and flour. After I closed the shop, I started taking it more seriously and built up a nice nest egg. And when the space elevator opened up a few years ago, demand for commodities exploded, and I found myself a wealthy woman."

"It's not fair," Kelly reacted angrily. "All those years you were calling me collect when I couldn't pay the rent on time and my apartment was playing mean tricks with the temperature. Were you laughing at me?"

"Oh, Kelly. Of course, not," her mother said in a soothing voice. "At first, I was trying to teach you to stop making impulse purchases, but for some reason, you always accepted the charges. After a while, I just hoped you'd figure out that it was cheaper to come home and visit us than to pay for all of the calls. But you always did the opposite of whatever I expected."

"Well, I'm ready for another beer," Joe said awkwardly in the pause that followed. "Who wants one?" Everybody at the table except for Dorothy and Jeeves raised their hands.

"Listen to this," Laurel said in the conversational lull, while they waited for Joe to return with a couple of pitchers. "Patches explained where his nickname is from. Tell them, Patches."

"It's not a big deal," the gangly youth mumbled. "I was just the first human to complete all of the Station Scout merit badges. When I sewed them all onto the uniform, there really wasn't any uniform left. So everybody started calling me 'Patches.'"

"I think it's sweet," Laurel said, appropriating his arm. "He even earned the merit badge for helping a Dollnick build a nest."

Everybody started pushing the embarrassed young man to describe his other meritorious activities, which turned out to include a surprising number of the inter-species equivalents to helping an old lady to cross the street. Kelly remained quiet, stealing an occasional glance at her mother, who was fully engaged by Dorothy's chatter.

"Libby?" Kelly subvoced.

"Yes, Kelly," Libby answered immediately over Kelly's implant. "Were you shocked by what Jeeves told you? Gryph and the others thought it came too close to giving away competitive business information about other species. But Jeeves insisted they aren't competing against Earth as much as they are competing against each other to attract capital from gullible humans."

"Oh, that," Kelly responded. "No, I don't care about that. I guess I'm just feeling stupid. Today I found out in front of my family and my friends that my mother is rich, and she called me collect all these years to teach me a lesson."

"You just won your bet with Blythe, figured out the Raider/Trader ties to the real economy, and you're calling yourself stupid?"

"I guess," Kelly replied vaguely. "Anyway, life should make a lot more sense from now on."

"Maybe you'll even stop talking to yourself," Libby added encouragingly. "You know, you forgot to schedule a week off from work while your mother is here. I arranged it with EarthCent, so you don't have to do anything other

200

than relax," the station librarian concluded and withdrew from contact.

Joe returned with two full pitchers of beer, and Kelly gladly accepted a refill as she tried to process everything that had just taken place. Looking on the bright side, her mother and Dorothy got along like a house on fire, so at least it meant a week without having to call InstaSitter.

Twenty-One

Kelly returned to the ice harvester after crying when her mother's passenger liner departed Union Station. She didn't know which of them had changed more with the years, but she no longer dreaded the idea of having her mother visit again. Kelly even promised to keep her eyes open for any good apartments that came up for sale in the human section.

Joe was sitting on the couch watching Dorothy play some incomprehensible game with Metoo when Kelly returned. Each player was equipped with a pile of colored slips of plastic that they added to a shared pile located between them, but Joe couldn't figure out the rules of order. Speed and accuracy of placement didn't seem to count for much either.

"Feel like a beer?" Joe asked her hopefully. Beowulf raised his head from the man's lap and added a pleading look to Joe's unsubtle hint.

"No, but I'll get you one," Kelly replied. "And some pretzels." Beowulf thumped his tail. She took Joe's glass, went down a level to fill it from the current keg, poured some mini-pretzels from a bag into a bowl, and returned.

"Aw, you didn't have to go to so much trouble," Joe thanked her, accepting the beer and the pretzel bowl. He usually ate pretzels out of the bag because it helped establish his dominance in the eyes of the giant dog. With the pretzels already in a bowl, who needed thumbs? Beowulf eyed the bowl speculatively, thinking pretty much the same thing.

Kelly sat on the arm of the couch, nibbled a few pretzels herself, and watched her daughter slap a blue slip of plastic on a pink one. "Good move," she called, not having a clue what was going on. Dorothy beamed back.

There was a polite knock on the open door of the ice harvester, and Dring appeared, carrying a copy of Trollope's novel, "The Way We Live Now."

"Dring, come in," Kelly rose and went to greet her reptilian friend. "How did you like the book?"

"Very enjoyable," Dring told her. "It reminded me of that amusing Grenouthian documentary about humans."

"Well, just remember that it's fiction, not history," Kelly replied defensively, though she couldn't have said why.

"And how were your mother's visit and your vacation?" Dring asked politely.

"Great," Kelly admitted. "Now that it's over, I can't believe I went so long avoiding my family. And taking a week off from those diplomatic dinners was a relief as well. Did I tell you that Libby worries I talk to myself? I'm beginning to wonder if it's the Stryx who are crazy. I don't talk to myself, do I?"

Dring looked away guiltily, and his tail gave a convulsive twitch, which Kelly had come to associate with embarrassment on the part of the dinosaur-like alien. Something about family and talking to herself clicked in Kelly's brain, and she maneuvered to put Dring between herself and Metoo. Then she stepped to the side, held up a hand, and called out, "Metoo! How many fingers am I holding up?"

Metoo looked up from the game and tilted his head in consternation. "You cut your arm off!" he exclaimed. Kelly quickly brought her arm out from where Dring was blocking the little Stryx's view of her hand, so that Metoo wouldn't get upset and put himself to sleep. "Oh, there it is. You aren't holding up any fingers," the little Stryx observed, then quickly returned to the game. Dorothy had taken advantage of Metoo's momentary inattention to recover some prize slips of plastic from the central pile, but if the Stryx had noticed, he didn't say anything.

Dring shifted uncomfortably and made a throat-clearing sound. Kelly waited for him to speak, but instead, he turned and waddled off in the direction of the book-shelves.

"Dring," Kelly said sharply. The alien turned towards her reluctantly. "They can't see you, the Stryx, can they!"

"We aren't invisible," Dring mumbled uncharacteristi-cally. "I was thinking of trying another Jane Austen. What would you recommend?"

"You didn't answer the question, Dring," Kelly rebuked him sternly. "I'll bet they can't hear you either. That's why Libby thinks I'm always talking to myself!"

"Well, technically they can hear us," Dring prevaricat-ed. "Technically, they can see us as well."

"How old are you, Dring?" Kelly asked directly.

"Very old?" he answered tentatively, as if he were the one asking the questions.

"As in, older than the Stryx?" Kelly pushed him.

"Not in this particular manifestation," Dring hedged. "Maybe I should just come back another time."

"You're one of their Makers, aren't you?" Kelly ex-claimed, an odd mixture of awe and accusation in her voice. "You didn't leave the Stryx and not tell them where you were going. You made it so they couldn't see you anymore."

"We asked them to ignore us," Dring admitted, his shoulders slumping as he capitulated. "I suppose they came up with the story that we went away and left them to explain it to themselves."

"Because you got bored with them?" Kelly asked incredulously, recalling Gryph's explanation of why the Stryx lost contact with their Makers.

"Nothing of the sort," Dring asserted, recovering a measure of his usual poise. "The Stryx turned out to be more interesting than our wildest dreams. They moved beyond our knowledge of science and technology so rapidly that we couldn't even begin to understand their innovations."

"I don't see the problem," Kelly said, with a look at Dorothy and Metoo. "Isn't being surpassed by one's children every parent's dream?"

"Surpassed, yes. Smothered, no," Dring replied sadly. "Imagine if Dorothy watched you every second of the day, rushing in to ask what you wanted if you made a motion to stand up."

"I could get used to that," Joe observed from the couch.

"Imagine if Dorothy watched you sleeping so she could wake you up if you had a bad dream," Dring pressed on.

"Yuck," Kelly acknowledged.

"Our Stryx would guess what we were thinking and supply the answers before we could even ask the questions. And if we refused their help, they were hurt, just like children. We tried to work it out between us for a long time, but they loved us too much to leave us alone. In the end, we had to ask them not to see us," Dring concluded sadly.

"But so many years have passed," Kelly argued. "And the Stryx are changing. Just look at Jeeves and Metoo."

"Yes, that's what brought me to Union Station and why I rented from Joe," Dring confessed. "Our people have always followed the Stryx closely, and I was delegated to come and investigate the changes and their relations with humans."

"Tricky bugger," Joe spoke from the couch. "And have you come to any conclusions?"

"My primary conclusion is that I'm not a very good spy," Dring admitted.

"I have diplomatic implants," Kelly pointed out. "My contract allows the Stryx to listen in on me all of the time. If I could guess who you are, I'm sure Libby or Gryph would have figured it out long ago just from my side of the conversation."

"It's not that they are blind to us or can't detect the sound waves we produce when speaking," Dring explained. "They selectively ignore anything that would make them aware of our presence. It's one of the advantages of a stable solution to the self-awareness equations that are at the heart of their artificial intelligence. They aren't bothered by the sorts of neuroses most biologicals would suffer in the same situation."

"Libby?" Kelly called suddenly. "Are you listening to this conversation?"

"I wouldn't call it a conversation," Libby responded over the ice harvester's speakers. "It sounds more like you've made a few random observations to Joe, who doesn't seem to understand what you're saying any better than I do."

"You mean I sound like an idiot," Kelly groused, with an evil look at Dring. "Thanks. I'll talk to you at work tomorrow."

"I truly am sorry about causing problems for you," Dring apologized. "I'd even be willing to reveal myself and try explaining it to your Stryx friends, but after all of these years, I don't know where to start."

"Start with him," Kelly said, pointing at Metoo.

Dring hesitated for a minute, and then he approached the children.

"Hello, Dorothy. Would you mind if I interrupted your game?"

"Hi, Uncle Dring!" Dorothy said, and looked up at the kindly dinosaur. "It's not a REAL game, we're just playing."

"Thank you," Dring replied. "Metoo," he spoke to the Stryx, who didn't appear to hear him. "You can see me if you want to."

Metoo looked up sharply and asked, "Where did you come from?"

"I've been here for some time, Metoo, and I've visited before. But I was hiding, like Dorothy's mother hid her hand earlier." The explanation was too complicated for Dorothy, but Metoo nodded his head gravely. "I helped make the original Stryx, a long, long time ago," Dring continued his explanation. "So I'm sort of a grandfather to you."

Metoo took the news in stride and didn't appear to be overly curious, but Dorothy jumped up and hugged Dring.

"You're Metoo's grandfather?" she asked excitedly, having understood that part of the conversation. "His family never visits because they're too big to fit!"

207

"Metoo is the offspring of Stryx Farth, who built Corner Station," Kelly interjected. "We explained to Dorothy that Farth would like to come and visit Metoo, but Corner Station is the same size as Union, so it wouldn't fit inside."

Dorothy ran from Dring to Metoo and whispered to the little Stryx, who nodded his head.

"Would you come with me to the next Parents Day at kindergarten?" Metoo asked Dring shyly.

Kelly waved frantically to catch Dring's attention and shook her head violently to warn him off. Dring didn't seem to understand her message, so she pantomimed putting her head in a noose and strangling, with her tongue sticking out and her eyes looking at the ceiling. Beowulf watched her reenactment of a hanging and gave a warning bark to cut it out.

"It would make me very happy to go with you, Metoo," Dring replied.

"Thank you, Grandpa," Metoo said politely, and then the children returned to playing as if nothing special had happened.

Dring approached Kelly with crocodile-sized tears running down his jowls. "I don't know how to thank you," he began. "No, no, don't brush it off. You can't imagine how exciting this moment is. That's the first time in history that one of our Stryx has ever asked us to do something for them!"

"Thank me after those kindergarteners get through with you," Kelly replied, disclaiming all responsibility. "You need to be a circus performer if you don't want them to eat you alive."

"It's not much better at the higher grade levels," Joe concurred ruefully. "If you don't have any special talents yourself, you can take Beowulf with you. Kids love dogs." Beowulf panted modestly.

"Special talents?" Dring asked, regarding Dorothy's parents with a twinkle in his eye. "Do you think this would be too shocking for them?"

Slowly, before their eyes, Dring's body began to change. Bumps appeared on his shoulders and his face began to elongate. He seemed to be going into a crouch, and his upper legs began to thicken as his finger and toenails grew into small claws. Triangular bumps began rising along his tail, and ridges formed above his eye sockets. In less than five minutes he was completely transformed into a small dragon, and when he spread his wings, they reached across the whole room.

After watching the metamorphosis, Beowulf yawned ostentatiously and gave him a look that said, "Is that all you've got?" Joe and Kelly were more impressed, both of them being struck speechless. Dorothy and Metoo looked up from their game when the breeze from the unfolding wings hit them.

"Uncle Dring!" Dorothy exclaimed, and jumped up to face the dragon. "Can I have a dragon ride?"

Metoo popped up right after her, calling, "Me too! Me too!"

Kelly finally found her voice and threw a wet blanket on the dragon party. "Not inside the house, children. Dring, can you still speak with us?"

Dring attempted to reply, but his words were accompanied by gouts of flame, and even Kelly's diplomatic grade implants failed to interpret the fluting sounds he made. Dring looked towards Metoo and nodded, and the little Stryx began to interpret for him.

"Grandpa says he can't change back here, so he's going to return to his ship for a while. He says that he'll tell everything to Libby and the other Stryx so they won't think you're going crazy and make you stop working for EarthCent. Grandpa says you're too good of an ambassador to risk losing."

With that, Dring folded up his wings, and with his claws clicking on the metal floor, hopped and waddled to the door of the ice harvester. From there he jumped into the air, spread his wings again, and soared lazily above the rows of mock-ups and shells and over the mound of scrap metal towards his home.

Joe rose laboriously from the couch and draped an arm around Kelly's shoulders. It wasn't clear if he was trying to support her or himself. Even Beowulf got up to watch Dring sail away, and as much as he hated to admit it, the old war dog was impressed. Dorothy and Metoo watched until Dring sank down below the pile of scrap, and then returned to playing with their plastic slips.

"Joe?" Kelly ventured, sounding suddenly young and vulnerable. "Do you think it's a coincidence that Dring looks just like a mythological creature from human fairy tales?"

"Stranger things have happened," Joe said. "Earth has been around for a few billion years, and the skies were full of flying dinosaurs a hundred and fifty million years ago. Who knows if some of them evolved into Dring and moved out into the galaxy before the ones left on Earth got wiped out. Maybe they go home to check in from time to time. Dring does seem to be the sentimental sort."

"I hope you heard him say that I'm too good of an ambassador to lose," Kelly hinted, recovering her equanimity.

"Alright, Beowulf is off the couch anyway," Joe replied with a sigh. "Lie down and I'll give you a foot massage."

Whimpering with pleasure as Joe rubbed her feet and she watched her daughter playing with Metoo, Kelly considered finally swallowing her pride and thanking Donna's daughters for pushing her blindly into marriage five years earlier. Then she remembered all of the InstaSitter commercials and decided it could wait.

EarthCent Ambassador Series:

About the Author

E. M. Foner lives in Northampton, MA with an imaginary German Shepherd who's been trained to bite bankers. The author welcomes reader comments at e_foner@yahoo.com.

You can sign up for new book announcements on the author's website - IfItBreaks.com